S

Prais

Frie

'Beau

Stor

'This

educ

Secr

'Def

neve

Tak

'Grip

story

Acr

'The

pove

Arr

'[Bri

fictio

Pawns

'… riveting and insightful.' *Sunday I*

BRIAN GALLAGHER was born in Dublin. He is a full-time writer whose plays and short stories have been produced in Ireland, Britain and Canada. He has worked extensively in radio and television, writing many dramas and documentaries.

Brian is the author of four adult novels, and his other books of historical fiction for young readers are *Friend or Foe*, set in Dublin in 1916; *Stormclouds*, which takes place in Northern Ireland during the turbulent summer of 1969; *Secrets and Shadows*, a spy novel that begins with the North Strand bombings during the Second World War; *Taking Sides*, about the Irish Civil War; *Across the Divide*, set during the 1913 Lockout, *Arrivals*, a time-slip novel set between modern and early-twentieth-century Ontario, and *Pawns*, set during Ireland's War of Independence. Brian lives with his family in Dublin.

Spies

Ireland's War of Independence

United friends ...
divided loyalties

Brian Gallagher

THE O'BRIEN PRESS
DUBLIN

First published 2018 by The O'Brien Press Ltd,
12 Terenure Road East, Rathgar, Dublin 6, D06 HD27, Ireland.
Tel: +353 1 4923333; Fax: +353 1 4922777
E-mail: books@obrien.ie
Website: www.obrien.ie
The O'Brien Press is a member of Publishing Ireland.

ISBN: 978-1-84717-980-7

7 6 5 4 3 2 1
21 20 19 18

Printed by CPI Group (UK) Ltd, Croydon, CR0 4YY
The paper in this book is produced using pulp from managed forests.

RENFREWSHIRE COUNCIL	
245272221	
Bertrams	15/08/2018
	£7.99
ERS	

Published in:

DUBLIN
UNESCO
City of Literature

DEDICATION

To Mark and Kate. Thanks for all the years of friendship.

ACKNOWLEDGEMENTS

My sincere thanks to Michael O'Brien for supporting the idea of a novel dealing with The War of Independence and Bloody Sunday, to my editor, Helen Carr, for her excellent editing and advice, to publicists Ruth Heneghan and Geraldine Feehily for all their efforts on my behalf, to Emma Byrne for her superb work on cover design, and to the everyone at O'Brien Press, with whom, as ever, it's a pleasure to work.

I'm grateful to Niamh Meddlar for her support, and to Ella Dermody and Daniel Barrett, young readers who shared with me their views of an early draft of the story.

My sincere thanks go to Fingal Arts Office for their bursary support.

And finally, no amount of thanks could express my gratitude for the constant support and encouragement of my family, Miriam, Orla and Mark, and Peter and Shelby.

PROLOGUE

THURSDAY SEPTEMBER 23RD 1920

THE MILL HOTEL, BALBRIGGAN,
NORTH COUNTY DUBLIN

Stella's pulses raced, her dream so vivid that she could almost smell the burning buildings as Balbriggan blazed. She thrashed about in her bed, living the horror again as she ran through the burning streets of the town. It was three days since the events had happened, but despite the terror she had endured, this was her first nightmare about it.

In her dream she sprinted towards the burning band hall, panting for breath as acrid smoke filled her lungs. Drunken Black and Tans – the mercenary police force that the British Government had drafted in to fight the Irish Republican Army – had set the town alight in revenge for the killing of two policemen.

Stella's father was an officer in the Royal Air Force, and her family was pro-British, but the Black and Tans behaved like thugs, and in her dream Stella feared that a drunken Tan might shoot her as she ran through the chaos. *But she had to get to the band hall.* It was where she played music each Friday night with her friends, Alice and Johnny, and now Johnny was in danger.

He had gone to the hall to get his precious clarinet, but hadn't returned. Had he been burnt in the fire? Shot by the Tans? Taken into custody? She *had* to find out, yet on reaching the back wall of the band hall Stella felt terrified by what she might discover. She forced herself to climb quickly over the wall and dropped down into the yard. Smoke billowed up into the night sky from blown out windows on the upper story of the building, and she felt a wave of heat as she ran towards the rear door. It was slightly ajar, and she quickly tied a handkerchief around her face, then stepped inside.

She was hit by a wave of heat and smoke, but she forced herself not to retreat. The collapsed ceiling had strewn the floor with rubble and heavy beams, and above her she could see that the fire was spreading through the top floor of the building. She picked her way carefully forward, then stopped dead. Through the swirling smoke she saw a body lying on the ground. The smoke thickened again, hiding it from view, but she had seen enough to horrify her. The body was Johnny's. Screaming in anguish, she ran towards it.

The scream jolted her awake, and Stella sat up in bed. She wasn't sure if she had just screamed in the nightmare or whether she had actually cried out. Her heart was thumping and her mouth felt dry. It would be embarrassing if she had woken anyone else in the hotel, yet even as she thought it she knew this was a trivial concern. People in Balbriggan had far bigger things to worry about. *She* had bigger things to worry about.

Johnny had survived the fire, after she revived him, but now he had left Balbriggan and Stella feared again for his safety. Although he was only fourteen, he had lived dangerously by working under cover for the rebels and, despite his brush with death three nights ago, she suspected he might take up the fight again in his new job in Tipperary.

Stella breathed out deeply, trying to still her racing heart. There was nothing further she could do for Johnny, except pray. And she had already prayed for him in her night prayers. Still, she wouldn't be going back to sleep any time soon. Maybe another couple of prayers would help. Lying in the dark, she blessed herself, joined her hands, and prayed hard that her friend would be safe.

PART ONE

SECRETS

CHAPTER ONE

RYAN'S BAR, THURLES, COUNTY TIPPERARY

SATURDAY, SEPTEMBER 25TH 1920

Johnny Dunne knew he was in trouble. He heard the trucks screeching to a halt in the street below, and his stomach tightened in fear. But he forced himself not to panic. He had seen enough Black and Tan raids to know he couldn't escape out the back door of the pub – the Tans would have men stationed there too.

The Black and Tans had come to Ireland the previous March to bolster the Royal Irish Constabulary in the war of independence that had raged for the last two years. The Tans had a frightening reputation for brutality, and Johnny didn't want to fall into their hands. As a fourteen-year-old he had been able to spy for the rebels all the previous year with few people taking notice of him. Until the previous week he had worked in Balbriggan's Mill Hotel, but he had left the town after the Tans ran riot, burning down dozens of homes, shops, and businesses, and killing two civilians.

Johnny had been ordered to move to a safe house in Thurles, while he awaited his next mission in Dublin. *So much for Ryan's Bar being a safe house*, he thought now, as he heard the Tans shouting and screaming as they burst into the pub. Johnny was two floors above them, in his bedroom, and he had a little time before they got to him.

Was there somewhere he could hide? There was no point hiding under the bed or in a wardrobe, the Tans were likely to look there. Johnny knew that Mr Ryan, the pub owner, was an IRA sympathiser, and that there were arms hidden on his farm outside the town. But if they found weapons here in the pub then anybody present would be interrogated. And Johnny couldn't allow himself to come to the attention of the Tans.

He thought frantically now as he heard more shouting and the sound of heavy boots pounding on the stairs. There was an attic above the bathroom across the landing, but the trapdoor into it was high above the floor. Maybe if he climbed onto the rim of the bath he could open the trap door, climb into the attic and hide till the Tans left? Unless they searched the attic too – in which case he would be found hiding, which would look extremely suspicious.

Johnny heard the pounding of the boots getting louder, and realised that the raiders had reached the first floor. He needed to make a decision, and quickly. Despite his fear, he tried to think clearly. With Mr Ryan hiding weapons at the farm, the chances were that he wouldn't risk also hiding arms here in the pub. The Tans, however, weren't to know that, so they might well search everywhere here, including the attic.

Better not hide at all, better to brazen it out, thought Johnny. He stepped across to the bathroom and flushed the toilet. He left the door open so that the sound of the flushing lavatory would be heard, then he quickly made for the stairs and descended.

He could hear the Tans in the first-floor living room shouting at Mr Ryan, and two of them faced him as Johnny reached the landing. One Tan aimed a rifle at him and the other man, who held a Webley pistol, grabbed Johnny and pulled him into the room.

'Where the hell were you hiding?' he demanded.

He was a heavily built man with reddish hair visible under his beret, and, to Johnny's surprise he had a Dublin accent. Most of the Tans were British, but Johnny had heard that there were Irish-men in their ranks also – men who were drawn by the generous wages the mercenary constables were paid.

'I was in the toilet,' answered Johnny, as he heard the sound of bottles being smashed in the bar below. Three more Tans ran up the stairs to the floor that he had just left. Another Tan roughly threw the furniture about the living room, then ran the bayonet of his rifle through the cushions on the sofa.

Although Mr Ryan was a tall, well-built man with a tough demeanour, he stood immobile, not complaining about the damage, and answering the Tans' questions. His eyes met Johnny's briefly and he gave the slightest of nods, as if to say things would be all right.

'What are you doing here?' asked the Tan with the rifle, and Johnny thought that his accent placed him from the north of England.

'I work here,' said Johnny. 'I help in the bar.'

'Live here too?'

'Yes, on the top floor.'

'Right vipers' nest of Shinners. You a little shinner too?'

If only you knew, thought Johnny. *If only you knew that Michael Collins, the Commander of the rebels, has a mission planned for me in Dublin.*

'I know nothing about politics,' said Johnny innocently. 'I'm just doing a job.'

'How come you've a job in Thurles? You're not from here, that's a Dublin accent,' said the red-haired Tan accusingly.

Always keep your lies close to the truth. It was what Johnny was taught when he had started spying for the rebels. 'Yes, I'm from

Dublin. But my da died, and we needed the money, so Ma got me this job through a cousin.'

Johnny could hear the Tans taking the place asunder above his head and he was glad that he hadn't hidden in the attic. Mr Ryan was still being questioned aggressively, but Johnny tried to block it all out and concentrate on his own situation. One slip here, one wrong word, and the game would be up.

'Where are you from in Dublin?' asked Red Hair.

'We live on the Northside,' answered Johnny, trying to sound as if he was co-operative, while still striving to be as vague as possible.

'*Where* on the Northside?'

'Phibsboro.'

'What street?'

Johnny hadn't expected the Tans to be this painstaking with their questions. His heart was thumping, but he barely hesitated, and came up with a road whose name had stuck in his memory.

'Monck Place.'

'House number?'

'Twenty-two,' said Johnny, not knowing how many houses there were in the street.

Was that the kind of thing the police checked in the aftermath of raids? He had no idea. But if they found his information was false they would assume that he lied for a reason. Then they would come looking for him.

The Tan wrote down the details that Johnny had given him. Did the man believe him? He seemed to. Then again, he could be playing cat and mouse. Johnny breathed deeply, forcing himself to appear calm. Meanwhile the Tan who had been bayonetting the cushions pulled the drawers out of a press, scattering the contents onto the floor, but without finding anything incriminating. All the time Johnny and Mr Ryan were held at gunpoint, then eventually the other Tans thumped back down the stairs, reporting that the attic and upper floor were clear. Without replacing the furniture or apologising in any way, the raiders prepared to leave. The Tan with the rifle pointed his finger at Mr Ryan.

'We found nothing this time, Paddy. Next time you mightn't be so lucky!'

Mr Ryan spoke calmly, but looked the man in the eye. 'My name isn't Paddy. And there's nothing illegal here, so luck doesn't come into it.'

Johnny saw a flicker of anger in the Tan's eyes, and for a second he feared that the man might strike Mr Ryan.

'OK, let's go,' said his red-haired companion.

The Tan stared hard at Mr Ryan, then turned away. As noisily as they had arrived, the raiding party took their leave.

Johnny breathed out, then turned to Mr Ryan.

'What time is the next train to Dublin?'

'Why?'

'I need to be on it,' said Johnny.

'They're not expecting you yet. There's a timetable for these things.'

'The Tans don't follow our timetable! They'll be back to arrest me if they check that address.'

'They'll hardly check an address a kid gave them in a raid.'

'I can't take that chance.'

'Look, I know we're an underground army, Johnny. But we're still an army. And your orders were to come to Dublin *when instructed*.'

'Yeah, and my orders were to stay in a *safe house*. But this house isn't safe any more. I'm no coward, Mr Ryan. I've taken risks for the cause. But I'm not hanging about to be picked up by the Tans. So, what time is the next train?'

Ryan seemed to consider this, then spoke resignedly. 'OK. There's a train at half-three. I'll tell Dublin you'll be on it.'

'Thank you. And Mr Ryan?'

'Yes.'

'Can I make a suggestion?'

Mr Ryan gave a crooked grin. 'Something tells me you will anyway.'

Johnny gave him a wry smile in return. 'If the Tans do come back, why don't you say you caught me with my hand in the till and sacked me? You don't know where I went, but you think I have relations in…will we say Cork?'

'Cork is a fine spot.'

'Cork it is, so. I'll start packing.'

Johnny turned away and made for the door, still feeling excited. Part of it was from the raid, and having outwitted the Tans. But part of it was thinking about what was to come. He would be working for his hero, Michael Collins, the most wanted man in Ireland. He took the stairs two at a time, eager to be on his way, and to start his new mission.

CHAPTER TWO

THE MILL
HOTEL,
BALBRIGGAN

SATURDAY, SEPTEMBER 25TH 1920

'Why are you being so snobby, Mam?' Alice Goodman looked at her mother who was sitting at the table in their private quarters. As the owner of the Mill, Mrs Goodman often ate in the hotel dining room. This evening, though, they were having tea in their quarters, and Alice had decided to challenge her mother's attitude. Three days previously Alice's friend, Johnny Dunne, had quit his job as the hotel boots, and ever since, Mam had been running him down.

'I'm *not* being snobbish,' said her mother. 'I'm simply saying that a boy with Johnny's background doesn't understand proper behaviour.'

Alice thought that Mam should be thanking her lucky stars that the Mill Hotel was still standing. Lots of buildings in Balbriggan were burnt-out ruins since the Black and Tans had run riot earlier in the week, yet here was her mother complaining about Johnny moving to a better job.

'There was nothing wrong with his behaviour, Mam. He always worked hard and was nice to customers.'

'That's not the issue. The point I'm making, Alice, is that a properly-reared boy, a boy from a good family, wouldn't just walk out on his employer.'

Alice kept her impatience in check and spoke calmly. 'It's not his fault he was raised in an orphanage, Mam. And the job he was offered in Tipperary had to be filled straight away.'

'So he gives one day's notice when he gets a better offer? I don't call that very loyal.'

'I don't mean to sound cheeky, Mam. But how loyal were you to him?'

'Excuse me?'

'Well, he wasn't exactly overpaid. And when he wanted to join the library, you didn't want to sign his guarantee. When he asked for one night off to play with the band in the music festival, you wouldn't let him go.'

'I needed him that night, Alice.'

'So, you put your business before him, and I understand that. But when he puts *his* business before *you*, you look down on him, and say he wasn't brought up properly.'

Alice could see that her mother didn't have a ready answer, and she decided to quit while she was ahead.

'Anyway, he's gone, so it's water under the bridge.'

'I suppose so,' conceded her mother.

'But what's going to happen to Balbriggan now?' asked Alice, deliberately changing the subject.

Her mother shook her head. 'I don't know. There's talk of a government enquiry into what the Tans did. And compensation for people who were burnt out. But no one knows how things will work out.'

Including me, thought Alice. Because in spite of defending her friend she too was concerned about how Johnny had left Balbriggan. She knew he had been spying for the rebels, and she feared that his sudden departure might be linked to that, despite the job in Tipperary.

She had never told her mother about Johnny's secret role. It was information that could spell disaster, as Alice feared her mother might feel obliged to tell the police that Johnny was working for the rebels. Only her best friend, Stella, knew of Johnny's secret life. But Stella hadn't been reassuring, and was as worried for Johnny's safety as Alice was.

'More tea, love?' said Mam now, breaking her reverie.

'Yes, please.'

Alice added some sugar, held out her china cup and smiled at her mother. Inside, though, she was still unsettled. Johnny had promised to write, but so far she had heard nothing. Was he really starting a job in Tipperary? Or was he resuming his role with the rebels? Or both? And if he was involved again, what would happen to him? She realised that there were more questions than answers, and she lifted her cup, sipped the hot, sweet tea, and tried to put Johnny from her mind.

CHAPTER THREE

NORTH BEACH, BALBRIGGAN

SATURDAY, SEPTEMBER 25th 1920

T he evening sun was dipping, its golden rays making the sea sparkle, but Stella Radcliffe barely noticed. Normally she would have relished a walk with her father along the shoreline, but tonight her mind was elsewhere.

Coming to Ireland from her native Canada a year and a half previously had seemed like an adventure, but the war of independence had changed things, and now Stella had conflicting emotions. She loved her father and felt a sense of loyalty to him. But Dad was a Wing Commander in the Royal Air Force, and Stella's support for the British forces had been changed by her friendship with Johnny Dunne. She had also grown to like the many Irish people she had met in school, and the chess club, and the town band, and she hated the way they had been treated by the Black and Tans.

'You're very quiet, Stella. Everything all right?' asked her father.

'I was…I was thinking about what happened.' Stella indicated the ruined buildings in the distance.

Her father shook his head. 'A bad business.'

'A bad business? They killed two men and destroyed half the town!'

'Sorry, poor choice of words.'

'They're not going to get away with it, are they, Dad? I mean, they will be punished, right?'

Her father paused, as though choosing his words carefully.

'There'll be an enquiry, Stella, I promise you that. And questions have already been asked. But as for the outcome…'

Stella stopped and looked at him. 'What are you saying, Dad?'

'It's…it's not cut and dried. There was chaos that night. It might be hard to pin down who did what.'

'They bayonetted two men! And burned buildings left, right and centre!'

'I know, darling, it's appalling. But civilised behaviour, law and order, all those things go out the window when you let slip the dogs of war.'

'The dogs of war?'

'It's a line from Shakespeare. It means unleashing the madness that war brings.'

'Right…'

'I saw it in France in the Great War, Stella. Some people will be noble and brave, but war brings out the animal in others.'

'But we're not at war, Dad.'

'I'm afraid we are, darling. Not like in the Great War, army to army. But there's still a war being fought here.'

'Against the people of Balbriggan?'

'I'm not justifying what happened, Stella. It makes me ashamed of my uniform when drunken thugs break the law. But I'd be misleading you if I promised that the men who ran amok will stand trial.'

Stella resumed walking, shocked by her father's words. No wonder the people of Ireland were increasingly supporting the rebels, she thought. She wished that Johnny was here so that they could discuss it. But Johnny was gone, and she didn't know when she would see him next. She hoped it would be soon. But even if she never saw him again he had been a great friend, and her proudest moment had been when she saved him from a blazing building.

'I know it's messy and difficult, Stella,' said her father. 'But whatever happens, we've got to get through this time as best we can. So any time you're worried, don't fret in silence. Come and talk to me, all right?

'All right, Dad.' She squeezed his arm and tried for a reassuring smile. Yet if she revealed her worries about Johnny that would,

29

in effect, be betraying him. She wished life could be simpler. She knew, however, that wishing was pointless, and so she linked her father and walked on wordlessly through the warm September evening.

Johnny realised he was in a city at war, as soon as he stepped out of Kingsbridge railway station. Two lorries full of heavily armed Black and Tans drove past the station entrance heading at speed in the direction of the Guinness brewery. On instinct Johnny averted his face and walked away, his head lowered as though his suitcase were weighing him down. The chances of the Tans looking for him in a follow-up to the raid in Thurles were remote. But in the lethal business of spying he knew that constant alertness was the difference between survival and disaster.

He crossed Kingsbridge, the sparkling waters of the River Liffey reflecting the glow of the setting sun, and the air heavy with brewing smells from the nearby Guinness plant. He looked downriver towards the centre of Dublin. The city was bathed in golden light, but the balmy atmosphere couldn't disguise the signs of conflict, and to his left Johnny could see the fortified entrance to the British army's Royal Barracks, overlooking the north quays. It was a large, imposing complex, and like the other barracks strategically situated around the city it bustled with activity in the escalating war of independence.

As he walked along the quays Johnny saw armoured cars, lorries full of British soldiers, and Auxies noisily raiding a pub at Chancery Street. The Auxies were a mercenary police force like the Tans, but were drawn from the ranks of former army officers, most of whom had been battle hardened in the Great War. Their reputation for brutality was as bad as the Tans, and Johnny gave them a wide berth as the made his way towards O'Connell Bridge and the city centre.

Although alert to danger, Johnny wasn't intimidated by the enemy. The British government had at its disposal the Royal Irish Constabulary, the British army, the Royal Air Force, and the Tans and Auxies, and yet the Irish Republican Army was successfully taking them on. And now he was going to play his part again in the fight for independence. It was thrilling to think that he would be working for Michael Collins, the most wanted man in Ireland. Though if he were honest, it was a bit daunting too, and as Johnny turned into Sackville Street, the city's main thoroughfare, he felt in equal parts nervous and excited at what lay ahead.

No use fretting about it, he told himself, the trick was to take it a day at a time. He passed the site of the General Post office, that had been ruined in the Easter Rising four years previously. Reaching into his jacket pocket, he took out two postcards. He had promised his friends Alice and Stella that he would write to them when he settled into the job that he had claimed to have down the country. Not wanting to give an address on a letter, he had instead bought two picture postcards of Tipperary beauty spots and written friendly messages on the cards while travelling to Dublin on the train. One postcard showed the Rock of Cashel and the other the Glen of Aherlow, and he slipped them into a pillar box, then continued up the street.

Much of the damage from the Rising had been repaired, and Johnny was impressed by the grandeur of the capital's widest thoroughfare. He crossed the street, leaving behind the imposing column that was Nelson's Pillar, which people claimed was the exact centre of Dublin. He made his way to the northern end of the street and continued into Cavendish Row. Before leaving Thurles, he had carefully studied a map of central Dublin, and Mr Ryan had pointed out exactly where he was to go. For security reasons nothing had been written down, but Johnny had memorised the address of the boarding house in Gardiner Place for which he was headed. He turned into Denmark Street and passed Belvedere College as the twilight began to deepen. Almost there, he thought, then up ahead he saw a row of tall Georgian houses and realised that had reached Gardiner Place. There were three adjoining houses with the name 'Hanlon' over the door of the central house, and Johnny mounted a short flight of steps.

He rang the bell, and a moment later the door was opened by a well-dressed woman of about fifty. She was slimly built, and had brown wavy hair that was flecked with grey. She looked at Johnny with clear blue eyes, and he sensed that this was a woman that you wouldn't want to cross. When she spoke, however, her tone was pleasant.

'Johnny Dunne, I presume?'

'Yes. Are you Mrs Hanlon?'

'I am indeed. Come in and take the weight off your feet.'

'Thanks.'

Johnny stepped inside and was ushered into a parlour and invited to sit in an armchair. The room was softly lit by a couple of lamps, and Johnny guessed that the rest of the boarding house would also be comfortable and clean, but not luxurious.

'Have you had anything to eat?' asked Mrs Hanlon, sitting opposite Johnny in another armchair.

'I had my dinner before leaving Thurles.'

'From what I've heard of growing boys, you'll be ready to eat again. When we're finished Bridget will get you a bun and a glass of milk.'

'Thank you. Who's Bridget?'

'She's in charge of the cooking here.'

'Right.'

'So, Johnny,' said Mrs Hanlon, 'you're an orphan.'

Johnny was taken by surprise. 'How did you know that?'

'Anyone who comes within an ass's roar of the Boss has to be checked out.'

'The Boss? You're…you're talking about Michael—'

'Don't mention names. Or even nicknames,' said Mrs Hanlon, cutting him short. 'I don't mean to sound rude, but we can't be too cautious. The Boss could refer to anyone, so that's what you'll call him.'

'All right.' Johnny looked at her appraisingly. 'So...you're not just a landlady?'

'I am to the public. Never give the slightest hint otherwise when we're outside this room, all right?'

'OK.'

'Good lad.'

'So what else have they told you about me?' asked Johnny.

'That you're brave. Cool under pressure. That you've provided good intelligence in the past. That you're from Dublin – though I would have known that.'

'From my accent?'

'And the way you carry yourself. Country people have a different way about them. You can learn a lot about people if you watch for the little clues.'

'I know,' said Johnny. 'I do that already.'

'Really?'

'Yes.'

'So what can you tell about me after two minutes?'

She said it with a hint of playfulness, but Johnny knew he was being tested. He thought for a moment, then spoke slowly. 'Because Mr Ryan told me, I know you're a widow,' he said, 'but I think you're a widow with no children. And I think you're from Kerry, but you've been living in Dublin a long time. And when you were in school, you were always one of the top pupils in your class.' Johnny sat back in his chair and looked at her enquiringly. 'How did I do?'

Mrs Hanlon nodded. 'You did well. Tell me your reasoning.'

'You said earlier "from what I've heard of growing boys, they're always ready to eat". But so are growing girls, and if you'd had either you'd know that. And we had a Christian Brother in the orphanage who was from Kerry, so I know the accent really well. Yours is the same as his, but less strong, so I guessed you've been living away from Kerry a long time. And because you own property here, I reckoned Dublin is where you've been living.'

'And the school?'

'For a woman to be working with…with the Boss…well, you'd have to be pretty smart. And someone that smart would have done well at school.'

Mrs Hanlon raised an eyebrow. 'I'm impressed, Johnny. You're sharp.'

'Thanks. I spent a year spying in the Mill Hotel – I had to be sharp.'

'What part of Kerry was the brother in the orphanage from?'

'I don't know. He wasn't…'

'Wasn't what?'

'He wasn't the kind of person you could ask. He…'

Johnny paused, and Mrs Hanlon leaned forward.

'He what, Johnny?'

'He had everyone terrified,' he answered reluctantly. 'He'd beat you around the place for the least thing.'

Mrs Hanlon looked pained. 'I'm sorry to hear that.'

'He wasn't even the worst.'

'Really?'

Johnny hesitated, then looked her in the eye. 'You might as well know. It was an awful place, a nightmare. They beat us, they fed us swill, we froze in winter. The reason I'm fighting for the cause is to make a different kind of Ireland.'

Mrs Hanlon nodded sympathetically. 'I understand that. I don't know why they'd want to treat children like that, but I understand your reaction. And for what it's worth, Johnny, I want a better Ireland too. Maybe together we can help bring that about.'

'I hope so. Can I…can I ask a question?'

'Of course.'

'What's happening about Mr O?'

Mrs Hanlon didn't answer at once, but Johnny sat forward in his chair, eager for an explanation. Over a year previously he had been recruited by Oliver O'Shea, a commercial traveller who visited the Mill Hotel, but who was secretly an intelligence officer for the IRA. O'Shea had recently been arrested at the hotel by the Tans, which was partly why Johnny had been ordered to leave Balbriggan.

'He's still in custody, Johnny.'

'When I was told to leave Balbriggan they said there were plans to free him.'

'You'll appreciate that I can't give details about that.'

'But he *is* going to be helped? Please, I need to know.'

'All right, Johnny. Yes, plans are afoot.'

'If there's any way I can help with that – any way at all – I'd like to.'

Mrs Hanlon looked thoughtful, then nodded her head. 'Good. We'll bear that in mind.'

'Thank you. And the job I'm in Dublin to do, can you tell me what it is?'

'Not tonight. Tomorrow is Sunday. Take the day off and relax. And then on Monday you'll be briefed.'

'What does that mean?'

'It means if you agree to what the Boss wants, your mission starts. Is that all right?"

Johnny felt his pulses starting to race but he tried to look calm. 'Yes,' he said. 'Yes, that's fine.'

CHAPTER FOUR

'Why are pirates great singers?' asked Mr Tardelli.

Alice turned in her school desk and looked at her friend Stella, who raised an eyebrow in surprise. Both girls really liked the Italian music teacher. With his flowing black hair and slightly Bohemian manner, he brought a touch of colour to their school, Loreto Convent Balbriggan. Mr Tardelli was also the musical director of the town band, of which the girls were enthusiastic members. It was part of the tradition of Friday-night band rehearsals that Mr Tardelli told jokes, but it was unusual for him to do so in the school setting, which explained Stella's surprise.

Alice, however, thought she understood his motive. Since the Black and Tans had run amok the previous week the town had been in shock. Life had to go on, though, and Alice reckoned that the Italian was doing his best to cheer up his pupils.

'Why are pirates great singers, Mr Tardelli?' she asked, deciding to show him some support.

'Because, Alice, they can hit the high Cs!'

The teacher was rewarded with a laugh from the girls, then he set them some work to practise before the next lesson, and the class broke up. The pupils quickly gathered their instruments and sheet music and made for the door. Before Alice could join the rush, Stella touched her on the arm.

'Can you wait for a second? We need to talk.'

'Of course.' Alice was intrigued and she sat back in her desk and waited until Mr Tardelli and the other girls left the classroom. They had just finished the final lesson of the day, and Alice wondered why Stella didn't simply chat to her as they walked home from school.

For the past six months Stella had had a room in the Mill Hotel that was owned by Alice's mother. Stella's own mother was nursing Granddad, who was sick in Canada, and her father was stationed with the RAF at Baldonnel Aerodrome. Between living under the same roof, going to the same school, and being members of the chess club and the town band, they had become best friends, and Alice hoped that everything was all right now.

'So what's up?' she asked when they finally had the classroom to themselves.

'Did you look closely at your postcard from Johnny?'

'Yes, it's a picture of the Glen of Aherlow.'

'Mine shows the Rock of Cashel,' said Stella. 'But it's not the picture that counts, it's the postmark.'

'How do you mean?'

'Why would I get a postcard from Tipperary, with a Dublin postmark?'

'I never looked that closely,' said Alice, turning her postcard over and scrutinising it.

'Neither did I until few minutes ago. Is yours postmarked Dublin too?'

Alice nodded. 'Yes. What do you think it means?'

'Maybe he's not in Tipperary. Or maybe he *was*, but now he's in Dublin.'

'But according to what he's written, he's working in Tipp.'

Stella nodded. 'That's the worrying part. If Johnny's misleading us, I can only think of one reason why.'

'You think…he's back working for the rebels?'

'I really hope not. I couldn't bear if anything happened to him'

'Me neither,' said Alice. Johnny had nearly been killed the previous week when the town was burned, and she dreaded to think of him surviving that, only to put himself at risk once more.

'If he's spying again,' said Stella, 'this is the kind of card he might send.'

'You think so?'

'Yes. To stop us worrying, and to make sure we're not linked to him if things go wrong and he's caught.'

'Could that be reading too much into it?' asked Alice. 'Maybe we're adding two and two and getting five.'

'So how do you explain the Dublin postmark?'

'Maybe he gave it to someone to post for him. Maybe they were coming to Dublin and posted it when they got here.'

'Possibly,' admitted Stella. 'And I'd love if that's it. But I'm worried that it's not.'

Alice looked at her friend. 'I hope you're wrong. But I've a bad feeling you're right.'

* * *

Johnny kept his eyes closed as he sat on his bed, softly playing the clarinet. Mastering the instrument had been the one good thing to come out of his time in St Mary's orphanage, and he had taken the clarinet with him when he left St Mary's the previous year. Despite the many adventures that he had while spying for the rebels in Balbriggan, he had always found time for music. Even when other developments were exciting – and meeting his hero Michael Collins today was a thrilling prospect – he could usually calm his mind by losing himself in the music.

Right now he was playing 'Gortnamona', one of Percy French's most-loved songs. The popular composer had died earlier in the year, resulting in a renewed interest in his work. Many of French's songs were lively and upbeat, but Johnny loved the haunting melody of 'Gortnamona' and he played it with tenderness. Suddenly his playing was interrupted by a knock on his bedroom door.

Johnny opened his eyes and put down the clarinet. His single bedroom on the first floor of Hanlon's Boarding House was small and plain, the only decoration being a crucifix over the bed and a drawing of an Irish Wolfhound on the wall. But it was spotlessly clean, the bed was comfortable, and he had settled in well since his arrival two days previously. This afternoon he had been told to be on standby, and now he had to make a conscious effort to control his excitement as he crossed the room and opened the bedroom door. Mrs Hanlon was on the landing, smartly dressed in an expensive looking coat.

'It's time, Johnny,' she said.

'Great.'

'Try not to look too excited. To anyone seeing us, we're just going about our normal business.'

'OK. Where are we headed?'

'Vaughan's Hotel. It's not too far.'

'Grand.'

Johnny closed the bedroom door and followed Mrs Hanlon down the stairs. They stepped out into Gardiner Place, and despite the hazy sunshine there was a nip of autumn in the air.

They began walking towards Denmark Street, and Mrs Hanlon spoke to Johnny in a low voice. 'What I said to you before, about security?'

'Yes.'

'You really need to take it seriously. Only today Countess Markievicz was arrested.'

Johnny knew that Countess Markievicz was a leading rebel who had fought in the Easter Rising. He looked at Mrs Hanlon anxiously. 'What was she arrested for?'

'We don't know the charge yet.

'Will that affect what we're doing?'

'No. Countess Markievicz will tell the police nothing. Besides, she doesn't know about what we're planning.'

'Right.'

'But the authorities are clamping down. You can't be too careful, Johnny. You mustn't breathe a word of anything you're involved in. Not to a soul.'

'Don't worry, I won't.'

They crossed to the far side of the road, heading towards the city centre, then after a moment Mrs Hanlon indicated to turn left into a narrow side street.

'Are we not going to Vaughan's Hotel?' asked Johnny, aware that the hotel's entrance was on Rutland Square.

Mrs Hanlon gave him a tight smile. 'There's more than one way into a hotel.'

They continued down a pungent laneway, then Mrs Hanlon suddenly stopped. Taking a key from her pocket, she opened a wicket gate in a large wooden door with VH written on it. 'Fewer prying eyes, this way,' she said, and she indicated for Johnny to follow her into a yard in which were stored wooden barrels and casks. She closed the wicket gate, crossed the yard, and entered a rear door to the hotel.

Johnny was tempted to ask how she got the key. But he remembered Mrs Hanlon's comments about security, and he said nothing. They came to a back stairs, and Mrs Hanlon immediately began ascending. So far they had encountered no hotel staff, but on the second landing a stocky, well-dressed man approached them. Johnny recalled the instruction to behave normally, and he tried to act like he and Mrs Hanlon were hotel guests heading back to their rooms.

The man looked him in the eye, and Johnny nodded pleasantly and said, 'Good afternoon.'

The man held his gaze, then smiled. 'He's a cool one,' he said to Mrs Hanlon. 'The Boss is expecting you.'

Suddenly the penny dropped, and Johnny realised the man was a bodyguard for Collins.

Before he could react, Mrs Hanlon crossed to a bedroom door, knocked twice and entered. Johnny followed her, excited that he was about to meet Collins.

The room they entered wasn't particularly large, but it had a table and chairs in a corner near the window. As Johnny closed the door a tall, well-built man with a neat moustache and sparkling eyes rose from his chair and came forward. He was wearing a collar and tie and a smartly cut suit, and he smiled and extended his hand.

'You must be Johnny,' he said, shaking hands firmly.

'Eh… yes,' answered Johnny, awestruck at meeting his hero, and not sure what else to say.

'Have a seat, please,' said Collins.

Johnny and Mrs Hanlon took two of the chairs, and Collins sat opposite them in the other one.

'I've heard good things about you, Johnny. You did well in Balbriggan.'

'Thanks.'

'We've another job in mind for you. But before we go into it, there's something I have to explain.'

'OK.'

'I know you took risks when you were gathering intelligence for Oliver O'Shea. But what we have in mind now…it could be more dangerous.'

'I'm not afraid of taking risks,' answered Johnny, his confidence boosted by the way Collins was taking him seriously. 'I'm a soldier fighting for Ireland – and all soldiers have to take risks.'

'Indeed. Though I'd prefer if young lads like yourself didn't do any soldiering.' Collins raised his hands in a gesture of apology. 'But we don't have the luxury of fighting the way we'd like to. The enemy has more men, more arms, more money, more equipment – so we use whatever we can.'

'I understand. Mr O'Shea explained it to me in Balbriggan.'

'Good.'

'But now we face a new threat, Johnny,' said Mrs Hanlon. 'Maybe the most dangerous we've ever faced.'

'Yes?'

'The one area where we've a clear advantage over the enemy is intelligence,' said Collins. 'We've sympathisers everywhere. Maids, barmen, taxi drivers, office clerks, you name it. They pass vital information up the chain to our intelligence officers. We couldn't take on the British without that information.'

'And now that's all at risk,' said Mrs Hanlon.

'How's that?'

Collins sat forward in the chair and spoke in a low, urgent tone. 'The British have sent a group of agents to Dublin. Their role is to wipe out our intelligence officers. If they succeed the war is lost. We've got to get to them before they get to us.'

Johnny was taken aback, but he tried to marshal his thoughts. 'So…where do I come in?'

'We know who these men are,' said Collins, 'but it's vital we track their movements.'

'You know who they are?' said Johnny, unable to keep the surprise from his voice.

'We've sympathisers in the police,' answered Collins matter-of-factly, 'and in the civil service, even inside Dublin Castle. So yes, we know who they are. But like I say, we need to track them. Where they go, who they meet, when they meet, what their routines are. We want you to help gather this information.'

'We've lined up a job for you as a messenger in the post office.'

'A telegraph boy can go anywhere without looking suspicious,' explained Collins. 'You can tail someone, then suddenly stop as though checking an address. It's the perfect cover.'

'We need to build up a detailed file on each of these agents,' said Mrs Hanlon. 'And the sooner the better.'

'Fine. When can I start?'

Collins smiled. 'I like your attitude, Johnny.'

Mrs Hanlon nodded her approval too. 'I'll talk to our contact tomorrow. You can probably start the next day.'

'Great.'

'There's one other job where we could use you,' said Collins. 'You said you'd like to help regarding Oliver O'Shea.'

'Absolutely! Are you going to try and spring him?'

'I can't go into details. Don't take offence, Johnny,' said Collins, but it's good security not to know more than you have to.'

'Sorry, I didn't mean to—'

Collins raised a hand to cut him off. 'It's all right. But if, for argument's sake, a rescue bid was happening – that would be riskier than tailing agents. In fairness, you need to know that.'

'It doesn't matter,' said Johnny. 'Mr O'Shea could have squealed on me when the Tans took him, but he didn't. So, please, count me in.'

'All right, we'll get back to you. That's everything settled, so.'

Collins stood, and Johnny realised that the meeting was over when Mrs Hanlon rose also. He quickly got to his feet as Collins approached smilingly.

'Good to have you on board, Johnny, we're in your debt,' he said shaking hands. 'I hope we can repay it someday.'

'I don't need paying, Mr Collins, I'm proud to play my part.'

'I know that, son.'

Johnny was about to go when a thought struck him. Michael Collins seemed to have contacts everywhere. Could he use that influence with the brothers at the orphanage? Johnny ached to know why he had been put into St Mary's, yet if he asked Collins to find out about his parents it might make him sound childish. *But he would never get a chance like this again.* Before he knew what he was doing he blurted it out. 'There is something,' he said, barely believing his own nerve.

Collins raised an eyebrow. 'Oh? What's that?'

'I really want to know who my ma and da were. Could you… could you find that out?'

Collins didn't reply at once, and Johnny feared that he had blundered in seeking a favour.

'I'm sorry,' he said, 'but…I just want to know what happened them.'

'I can't make a promise on something like that,' said Collins.

Johnny tried to hide his disappointment. 'Well…sorry for asking.'

'But I'll have it looked into. Leave it with me.'

'Thank you so much!' said Johnny.

Collins gave a friendly nod of farewell, then Johnny found himself out on the landing with Mrs Hanlon.

'Where did that come from about your parents?' she asked.

'I don't know. It's something that's nagged at me for ages.'

'Well, if we can help, we will. But your priority now is your new job. Agreed?'

'Absolutely,' answered Johnny, then he nodded to the bodyguard on the landing and happily followed Mrs Hanlon down the back stairs of Vaughan's Hotel.

CHAPTER FIVE

lice felt like kicking herself. She was playing chess with Stella in front of a log fire in the sitting room of her family quarters in the Mill, and she had just made a bad move. Sure enough, Stella spotted her mistake and quickly took her castle. Alice told herself to concentrate, though she knew that she was never going to be able to give her full attention to the game.

In reality, the chess match was a cover, to provide Alice and Stella with a chance to use the Goodman's private telephone line as soon as Alice's mother left. As the owner of the Mill Hotel, Mrs Goodman had status in Balbriggan, and tonight she was to attend a meeting for business people who wanted to regenerate the town after the disastrous fires of the previous week.

Alice tried to focus on the game. She told herself that Stella must be just as distracted as herself. Maybe even more so, as Stella was the one whose suspicions had been aroused by the Dublin postmarks on Johnny's cards from Tipperary. And despite being the daughter of a serving RAF officer she was particularly close to Johnny, having saved his life the night that the Tans had gone on the rampage. Alice suddenly wished that he was still here. Stella was a great friend, and they had good fun together, but she really missed Johnny – they both did. Alice looked down at the chess board, recalling how skilful a tactician Johnny was. Maybe that tactical skill would help him to evade capture, if he was working again with the rebels. Alice's musings were suddenly cut short when her mother came into the sitting room.

'I'm heading off now, girls,' she said, buttoning up her overcoat.

'See you later, Mrs Goodman,' said Stella.

'Have you finished all your homework, Alice?'

'Yes, Mam. And I'll brush my teeth and wash behind my ears!'

Her mother smiled and kissed her on the forehead. 'I shouldn't be too late.'

'OK, bye.'

Mrs Goodman left, closing the door behind her.

'I can't think of chess for another second!' said Stella, rising and turning away from the board.

'I'm glad it's not just me,' said Alice with a grin as she too stood up. 'But let's give it a minute, in case Mam forgot anything or pops back for some reason.'

'All right.'

'What was the exact wording again on your card from Johnny?' asked Alice. 'The part about work?'

Stella took the postcard from her pocket and read. 'Very busy settling in to the new job, will write when things quieten down.'

'OK, there's no two ways about it. He should be busy working in the pub in Tipp.'

'And maybe he is,' said Stella. 'I sure hope so.'

'Let's find out.'

The two girls turned away from the chess set and crossed to the polished sideboard where the telephone stood. Alice's plan was based on the fact that although Johnny had been vague about his location, she had a clue to his whereabouts. Before leaving Balbriggan, Johnny had claimed that he was being met at the train in Thurles and didn't know the precise address of his future employer. But on secretly slipping a parting gift into Johnny's jacket pocket, Alice had seen the name Ryan's Bar written in Johnny's hand on a sheet of paper. If the telephone operator had a listing for a Ryan's Bar anywhere near Thurles, it might be possible to make contact with their friend.

'I'm kind of nervous,' said Alice, 'now it's come to it.'

'Just ring as though it's the most natural thing in the world.'

'All right.'

'Do you want me to do it?' asked Stella.

Alice was tempted to relieve herself of a tricky undertaking. But Stella had a clipped Canadian accent, and Alice reckoned that someone with an Irish voice might stand a better chance of getting information. 'No, it's OK.'

Alice lifted the handset, then dialled for an operator. She turned to Stella, and with her free hand crossed her fingers. Stella nodded encouragingly and gave her a thumbs-up.

Suddenly a woman came on the line, 'Hello, caller, what number do you require?'

'I'm looking for Ryan's Bar in Thurles, County Tipperary, please,' said Alice, in the most confident tone she could muster.

'One moment, please.'

Alice found herself holding her breath and she forced herself to breathe deeply. Her heart quickened as she rehearsed in her head what she was going to say. After a few moments there was a click on the line.

'Putting you through, caller,' said the operator.

'Thank you.'

There was a ringing tone, and Alice swallowed hard, more nervous than she had expected to be. The call wasn't answered, however, and Alice found her nervousness being replaced by frustration. *Come on*, she thought, *pick up the phone!*

'No luck?' said Stella, when it continued to ring out.

'No.'

Alice was about to replace the handset when a male voice came on the cackly line.

'Hello?'

'Hello,' said Alice excitedly, 'is that Ryan's Bar?'

'Yes, this is Ryan's.'

'Ryan's Bar in Thurles?'

'No, Ryan's Bar in Kathmandu!'

'What?'

'Yes, Ryan's Bar in Thurles.'

Alice realised that she had sounded foolish, and she gathered herself briefly before continuing.' I'm looking for Johnny Dunne, please.'

There was a slight pause, then the man answered. 'Sorry, no Johnny Dunne here.'

'Are you sure? Johnny Dunne, recently arrived from Balbriggan.'

'Say you're a friend,' suggested Stella in a whisper.

'I'm Alice Goodman, a friend of his, and I just wanted a quick word,' added Alice, trying to make her tone sound reasonable.

'Like I say, there's no Johnny Dunne here.'

Something in the man's answer sounded shifty, and on instinct Alice became more assertive. 'But he was there, wasn't he? He *told* me he was going to Ryan's Bar in Thurles,' she improvised.

There was a pause. 'He was here briefly,' the man conceded. 'But he's left for another job.'

I knew he was fobbing me off, thought Alice. 'Have you got an address where I can contact him, please?'

'No, he didn't give an address.'

'He must have said something about where he was going.'

Again there was a slight pause, then the man spoke. 'He mentioned something about Cork. But that's all I know.'

'Maybe Mr Ryan would have an address,' suggested Alice, hoping that there might be an owner who knew more than this man.

'I *am* Mr Ryan. And I've no forwarding address. Sorry.'

Before Alice could question him further the man hung up, and the line went dead. Alice slowly put down the handset as Stella looked at her enquiringly. 'He claims that Johnny has moved on. That he mentioned going to Cork.'

'He gets a new job, but only stays a couple of days?' said Stella disbelievingly. 'And he goes to Cork – where there'd be plenty of post-boxes – but his cards are posted in Dublin?'

'I know,' said Alice. 'It doesn't hold up.'

'I think either Johnny lied, or that man did.'

'Yeah,' said Alice. 'And either way, it's not good, is it?'

'We don't want slackers, we don't want messers; one wrong move and you're out on your ear. Got that?'

'Yes, sir,' said Johnny. He was being briefed by Mr Williams, the supervising despatcher in the Post Office's Telegraph Service. The General Post Office building on Sackville Street had been destroyed in the 1916 Rising, and the telegraph service had moved to temporary premises while rebuilding work went on. Soberly dressed telegraph clerks sat at serried rows of long benches, receiving incoming telegrams and sending outgoing ones, and Johnny liked the hum of the wires, the clacking of the machines, and the sense of being at the centre of communication from all over Ireland. Bright morning sunlight streamed in through the windows now, but now Johnny's focus was entirely on the man opposite him.

'Delivering telegrams is a responsible job,' said Williams sternly. 'If you're honest and hardworking you could do well. If you step out of line, there're no second chances, you'll be gone.'

'I understand,' said Johnny.

They were at the telegraph despatcher's desk, and Johnny nodded respectfully at the supervisor. He was a plump man in his fifties, conservatively dressed in a dark grey suit. Johnny, however, knew that his strict manner was for the benefit of a clerk who was working nearby. Sure enough, the supervisor's demeanour changed when the clerk moved off.

'You'll work like a normal delivery boy and you'll be paid the usual wage,' Williams said, in a warmer tone, and with his voice lowered. 'But most days there'll be orders about who we want you to tail. You'll fit that in between your regular duties, OK?'

'OK.'

'All these men you follow have military backgrounds. And some of them are experienced agents. Don't underestimate them.'

'I won't,' said Johnny.

'Be sure you don't. They're dangerous.'

Johnny felt a hint of butterflies in his stomach, but he kept his face impassive.

'And if you have to choose between losing someone that you're tailing, and risking being noticed – better to lose them.'

'All right.'

'Having said that, your uniform, and the post office bike, make you semi-invisible. Most of the time you'll blend easily into the background. Mrs H tells me you've been getting familiar with the city?'

'Yes. I knew it a bit already, and I've been studying maps and walking around the city centre.'

'Get to know it like the back of your hand,' said Williams emphatically. 'We don't have many advantages over the enemy. Knowing the battleground inside out needs to be one of them.'

'Once I'm given the bike this morning I'll cycle everywhere. And after work each day I'll explore the city, till I know every nook and cranny.'

'Good lad,' said Williams, 'All right, go in to the depot now and get issued with your bike. Then come back to me and I'll give you some telegrams to deliver.'

'And the other work?'

'That starts this afternoon. There's a Lt. Colonel Jennings we're interested in. He's booked a lunch table in the Gresham Hotel. When he comes out, we want you to check where he goes and who he meets.'

Johnny felt his pulse starting to race, 'How will I know what he looks like?'

'He'll be pointed out to you.'

'Fine.'

Williams offered his hand. 'Good luck, son.'

'Thanks,' said Johnny, shaking hands. Then he headed off to get his new bike, pleased that the waiting was over, and ready to start his mission.

CHAPTER SIX

'Why do humming birds hum?' asked Mr Tardelli. He looked enquiringly at the assembled band members with a twinkle in his eye as they took a break during Friday night rehearsals.

'Why do I know this will be a terrible joke?' Alice whispered to Stella, but before Stella could reply Mr Tardelli delivered the punchline.

'Because they don't know the words!' he said.

In spite of themselves the girls laughed, and Stella admired the band leader for his efforts to lift everyone's spirits. It had been a difficult ten days for the people of Balbriggan, what with the funerals of the people killed the night of the fire, and the need to house those whose homes were in ruins. Gradually, however, life was returning to normal, and Stella was glad that the band had resumed practising. Two of the band members had had their homes damaged in the fires, but for a couple for hours tonight Mr Tardelli was transporting everyone to a happier place.

The band hall from which she had rescued Johnny had been destroyed, but the bandmaster had arranged for them to use a church hall on a temporary basis. They all took their positions now as the rehearsal began again, and Stella picked up her violin.

'OK, we play "Let the Rest of the World go by",' said Mr Tardelli.

'And please, no *staccato*. This is a melody that *flows*.'

'From your soul, Stella, let the melody flow!' whispered Alice in a good impersonation of the bandmaster's Italian accent.

Stella smiled, then placed the violin to her cheek. On a signal from Mr Tardelli they began to play, and Stella tried to lose herself in the sweep of the music. Usually she could leave her worries behind and get caught up in her playing, but tonight reality kept intruding.

Three days had passed since the phone call to Ryan's Bar in Thurles, and no further correspondence had come from Johnny. She hoped against hope that he wasn't involved again with the IRA. Any kind of rebel activity was more dangerous now, with the RIC re-enforced by large numbers of Tans and Auxies. Balbriggan almost felt like an armed camp, and far from being apologetic in the aftermath of setting the fires, the Tans were as aggressive as ever.

With each passing day, Stella had found her allegiances shifting away from the authorities and towards the rebels. She felt guilty at being sympathetic towards a rebel victory, and part of her still respected her father's dedication to the rule of law. Most of the RAF officers she met through Dad seemed honourable and pleasant, but the behaviour of the Tans and Auxies made a nonsense of the notion of law and order.

Stella played on, one part of her brain producing the music, while the rest of her mind was distracted.

'Penny for your thoughts,' said Alice when they had finished the tune.

'Is it that obvious I'm distracted?'

'You just looked like you were away with the fairies!'

Stella smiled ruefully. 'I was thinking about this sports day in Lusk next weekend. Dad doesn't want me to attend.'

'I can see why he mightn't,' answered Alice.

Although the sports day was a charity event to raise funds for those who had lost their homes and businesses in the torching of the town, Stella knew there was also an element of anti-government protest involved.

'So what will you do? asked Alice.

'I'm going to go anyway. What the Tans did was criminal, and I've no problem with people knowing I think that.'

'Good for you.'

'All right,' cried Mr Tardelli. 'We play "Give My Regards to Broadway". With energy please! *Con brio!*'

'OK, this one's tricky,' said Alice. 'Better forget all that stuff and concentrate on the music.'

'Right.'

Stella returned her attention to her sheet music, and the rehearsal continued, with the evening finally coming to a close with a rousing rendition of one of her favourite pieces, '*Funiculi, Funicula*'.

The two friends made their way out of the church hall, then Stella stopped dead on seeing her father waiting at the door.

'Commander Radcliffe,' said Alice.

'Girls.' He nodded in greeting, but Stella feared from his unexpected presence and grave expression that something was wrong.

'Dad. Is…is something up?'

Before her father answered, he turned to Alice.

'Could you…could you excuse us for one moment please, Alice?'

'Of course.'

Stella felt a sinking feeling as Alice moved off to chat with some of the other band members. 'What's wrong, Dad?' she asked.

'I've just got a telegram from Mum. I'm sorry to tell you… Granddad has taken a turn.'

'Taken a turn? What does that mean?'

'He's…he's slipped into a coma.'

'Is he going to die?'

'I'm afraid so, darling.'

Stella felt her mouth go dry, but she forced herself to ask the question that terrified her.

'Will he…will he die tonight?'

'We don't know. Probably not – sometimes people linger in comas for weeks. But the end is coming. I just thought you should know.'

'Thanks, Dad.'

Stella felt her eyes welling with tears, and her father wordlessly reached out and took her in his arms. Ever since her mother had returned to Canada to nurse Granddad she had known this day was coming. But now that it had arrived it still took her by surprise, and she stood unmoving, the tears rolling down her cheeks as she sobbed softly in her father's arms.

Johnny's heart began to thump as Mrs Hanlon approached him. He was at the sunlit corner of Gloucester Street, and she had exited the main door of the Gresham Hotel into Sackville Street. Johnny was sitting astride his post office bike, dressed in his new work uniform. Nobody had paid attention to him as he had appeared to sort through telegram envelopes. He slipped the envelopes into his satchel now as Mrs Hanlon drew near. She was smartly dressed for her visit to the Gresham Hotel and, though she walked casually, Johnny suspected from the look in her eyes that she was excited.

'We're on!' she said quietly, pausing briefly beside Johnny on the pavement and seeming to adjust her hatpin. 'Don't stare, but Lt. Colonel Jennings is the man in the navy suit who's just walked out of the hotel.'

Johnny glanced back towards the Gresham Hotel. He saw that his target had turned away and was starting to head south along Sackville Street towards the river.

'Remember all I said when you're trailing him,' said Mrs Hanlon, not looking at Johnny, but appearing to wait for a break in the traffic in order to cross the road.

'I will.'

'Good luck.'

'Thanks.' Johnny mounted his bicycle and turned into Sackville Street. He cycled slowly and began to close the gap on his target. Lt. Colonel Jennings, he noted, walked with an easy confidence but didn't draw attention to himself in any way. His suit appeared well-cut, but not flashy, and to all outward appearances he seemed like a respectable gentleman going about his business.

Johnny slowed down, not wanting to overtake the British officer. He had agreed with Mrs Hanlon on a technique for following his quarry. If he were tailing targets that were on foot, he couldn't cycle all the time without repeatedly passing them and having to stop. And so they had devised a system whereby Johnny would cycle some of the time, walk wheeling the bicycle at other times, and sometimes stop completely while appearing to sort through his telegrams. He put it into practice now, never overtaking Lt. Colonel Jennings, but never allowing him to get too far ahead either.

Jennings picked up his pace a little and within a few moments they had passed the partially rebuilt GPO and reached the broad expanse of O'Connell Bridge. Johnny slowed down, realising that Jennings was about to cross the River Liffey to the south side of the city. The tide was out, and Johnny's nostrils were assailed by the smell from the exposed river bed.

Ignoring the foul smell, Johnny waited until his target was approaching the junction of Burgh Quay and Westmoreland Street, and mounted his bicycle again and began to cycle after him. He pedalled easily, then glancing ahead, he got a shock. Esther Moore, one of the girls who had played with him in the Balbriggan Town Band, was walking across the bridge with her mother. Johnny didn't think she spotted him and he quickly lowered his head and accelerated towards Westmoreland Street. Esther didn't call out his name as he sped past, and on reaching the southside and drawing close behind Jennings again he slowed down. He breathed out, relieved that Esther didn't seem to have seen him, then he concentrated once more on tracking his target.

The near miss was a valuable lesson, he thought, as he followed Jennings towards Trinity College. *You could never tell what development might suddenly throw you. Every moment spent working for the rebels required alertness.*

More on guard than ever, he followed Jennings as he made his way up Grafton Street. It was the city's most fashionable thoroughfare, and well-heeled Dubliners were doing their Saturday shopping in its many stores and coffee shops. Yet there was no getting away from the sense that Dublin was a city in strife. Already Johnny had seen Tans mounting a checkpoint at Abbey Street, and two armoured cars driving along Dame Street, and now a heavily armed patrol of Auxies was making its way down Grafton Street. People quickly got out of their way, and Johnny watched carefully to see how his quarry reacted to them.

Jennings, however, walked past the men without glancing in their direction. It wasn't that surprising, Johnny thought – an experienced officer was hardly going to advertise his allegiance by interacting with Tans or Auxies. Johnny continued his technique of cycling, wheeling his bike and occasionally stopping, and after a few more minutes his target reached the top of Grafton Street and entered the oasis of St Stephen's Green.

Johnny dismounted and followed him at a distance, the bustle of the city fading away as Jennings moved deeper into the park. There were lots of people about, and the park looked resplendent, its trees beginning to turn gold with the approach of autumn.

Johnny tailed his quarry along the side of the ornamental pond, then Jennings sat on a bench that was occupied by another well-dressed man. Hanging back, and once more pretending to sort his telegraphs, Johnny observed the man carefully. Mrs Hanlon would want an accurate description, and Johnny noted that the second man was heavy-set and had a neatly trimmed black beard.

The conversation between the two men was brief, but Johnny watched intently and spotted it when Jennings passed an envelope to the other man. Was Blackbeard an informer who was being paid? Or perhaps he was Jennings's controller, receiving a report? Either way, Johnny knew that this was exactly the kind of information that he was meant to gather.

Their short conversation over, the two men parted, and Johnny followed Jennings again, always at a discreet distance. Nothing further of importance happened, however, and he tracked his target out of the park and all the way to Leeson Street without incident.

Without warning the British agent turned into the entrance of a hotel. Johnny had been told that if something like this happened he was on no account to follow Jennings inside. Instead he continued cycling normally, noting that the hotel was called the Eastwood Hotel. At the next junction he turned left, then he began the journey home, excited at having carried out his first mission.

CHAPTER SEVEN

'Stella!' cried Alice, crossing the noisy schoolyard. It was the first morning break at Loreto Convent, and Alice made for her friend, hoping to lift her spirits. Monday morning was always a bit lack-lustre, but this morning Stella had been more downbeat than usual. It was hardly surprising, Alice thought, what with her grandfather being ill in Canada. Alice and her mother had prayed for him at Mass the previous day, but Stella had said that Granddad was in a coma and wasn't expected to regain consciousness. Now as Alice drew near her friend, she was excited to have news that should distract her.

'What is it?' said Stella.

Alice realised that her excitement must be showing. 'You're not going to believe this,' she said.

'Try me.'

'I bumped into Esther Moore at the toilets.'

'And?'

'She said she saw Johnny on Saturday.'

Stella looked startled. 'Really? Where?'

'In Dublin. Esther went up on the train with her mother. She saw Johnny on O'Connell Bridge.'

'And she's sure it was him?'

'Certain.'

'Did she talk to him?'

'No, she couldn't. He was working.'

Alice could see that Stella was taken aback, but at least the news had shaken her friend from her melancholic mood.

'So the postcards from Tipperary *were* a red herring,' said Stella.

'Looks like it. Though in fairness to Johnny, he wouldn't lie to us unless he really had to.'

'When you think about it, that's not reassuring.'

'No, I suppose not,' conceded Alice.

'What was he working at?'

'Esther said he was in the uniform of a telegraph boy.'

'Yeah? How do you suddenly go from a bar in Tipperary to delivering telegrams in Dublin? And if there's a good reason, why lie to us?

'We could...we could always ask him,' suggested Alice.

'How?'

'We know where he works now. If we went to Dublin next Saturday we could visit the telegraph office. We could say we've an important message for Johnny Dunne, and we need to see him.'

Stella looked thoughtful, and Alice knew that her friend's mind was racing. Even though the news about Johnny was worrying – Alice feared he *was* involved again with the rebels – it was still good to see Stella more animated than she had been since getting the news about her grandfather.

'What do you think?' asked Alice.

'We'd have to come up with a story, to get permission to go to

Dublin.'

'So we'll invent something. And we'll promise to be careful and all that. But you're on to try and track him down?'

Stella nodded. 'I hope there's an innocent explanation. But if not, and he's with the rebels again, I need to know.'

'Me too.'

'Let's do it then.'

'Right,' said Alice. 'We'll make up a story, and go to Dublin on Saturday.'

Johnny strode along Dorset Street. The dog he was exercising pulled him ahead, straining at the leash. It was a cool autumn morning, and it was a novelty for Johnny to walk a dog, something he had never done in either the orphanage or when working at the Mill Hotel. It was a change too to be dressed in high-quality clothes, but Mrs Hanlon had kitted him out in an expensive boy's suit and a smart gaberdine overcoat. She had explained that in today's bid to rescue Mr O'Shea, Johnny's role would be to pose as a posh schoolboy.

Johnny was excited to be involved, and flattered that he had been given a key task. He knew that Mrs Hanlon had been pleased with his tracking of Lt. Colonel Jennings three days previously, but it was still a boost to his ego to be trusted in the attempt to free Mr O'Shea.

'Easy, Rex!' he cried now as they turned into Western Way and the dog tried to surge ahead. He made his way expectantly towards Broadstone Railway Station. In the ten days since moving to Dublin he had settled well in the boarding house, started his cover job delivering telegrams, tracked British agents around the city, and now he was preparing to help free a prisoner.

It was lonely not having friends to talk to, but he accepted that that was the price of serving Michael Collins. On several occasions he had played football on the street with boys from nearby Mountjoy Square, but he knew that for the next couple of months he couldn't get too friendly with anyone – not while carrying out his mission. He drew nearer the station now, his excitement building. *Calm down*, he told himself, *nothing will be happening just yet*. Still, it was better to be in place in plenty of time. And part of the plan called for the dog to be straining at the leash, so he didn't want to tire him out by walking for too long.

He looked at the animal admiringly. It was a large German Shepherd, fully grown, but still young enough to be energetic. In one way it was surprising that he had been provided with a German Shepherd. Mrs Hanlon had told him that Michael Collins was a dog lover who was promoting the breeding of Kerry Blues. For years the Irish Wolfhound had been the dog associated with Ireland, but the British Army had adopted the wolfhound as the mascot of their Irish Guards, and so Collins had championed the Kerry Blue as the breed to represent the new, nationalist Ireland.

For the rescue plan, however, they wanted a dog that would be big and obvious, and so a sympathiser had lent Rex for today's mission. The mission itself involved risk, but Johnny saw that they had chosen a good spot to carry it out when he arrived at the junction of Western Way and Constitution Hill. A vehicle coming up the hill wouldn't be travelling at high speed, and the road narrowed where the Foster Aqueduct carried the Broadstone Branch of the Royal Canal over the road and into Broadstone station. Broadstone Harbour had long since been filled in, and the former aqueduct was now just a bridge, but it was a pinch point at the top of Constitution Hill, and Johnny admired the planning that had gone into choosing the site for the rescue bid.

Mrs Hanlon had explained that their informants in the legal system had tipped them off that O'Shea was being sentenced this morning. The shortest route from the courts to Mountjoy Prison was via Constitution Hill and Phibsboro Road, and so the plans had been made accordingly.

Johnny loosened the lead slightly and allowed the dog to pull him. He started down Constitution Hill towards the gardens of the Kings Inns law complex, then met Mrs Hanlon as she strolled out the gate. She stopped and admired the dog, quietly speaking from the corner of her mouth.

'You're early, Johnny.'

'I know.'

'Stroll around for a few minutes, but don't wander off. We've someone on a motor bike who'll let us know when they've left the courthouse.'

'OK.'

'Right. Good luck, then.'

'You too,' said Johnny, then he loosened the lead again and let the dog pull him away.

The October air was gusty, with the first leaves of autumn swirling along the ground. Johnny had been glad to wear the heavy gabardine overcoat, but now he felt a film of perspiration on his brow. He lifted the expensive schoolboy cap that he was wearing and mopped his brow.

What had felt like the longest half hour of his life had elapsed, but now the advance warning had been given by the motorbike rider, and Johnny walked with the dog towards the Foster Aqueduct. Roadworks were being carried out, and a large group of workmen were digging up the nearby pavement. Johnny swallowed hard, knowing that he had to get the timing of his move just right if the plan was to work. He stopped at the side of the path, reining in the dog. Mrs Hanlon stood beside him, appearing to chat to another woman that he had never seen before.

Johnny heard the sound of approaching engines, then Mrs Hanlon spoke in a soft but urgent tone.

'We're on, Johnny, this is them!'

'OK.'

Johnny looked down Constitution Hill and saw two black

police vans climbing up the hill. Just as they were reaching the summit he flicked the leash. 'Go, Rex!' he said.

The German Shepherd didn't need further encouraging. He immediately lunged forward, appearing to pull Johnny out onto the roadway after him. Johnny knew that everything depended on the split-second impression that the driver of the first van got. Would he see an immaculately dressed, respectable boy whose dog had pulled him into danger – in which case he would surely brake? Or would he be on guard for an ambush and liable to accelerate around Johnny or perhaps even at him?

Johnny's every instinct was to get out of the way of the van, but he forced himself to pull on the leash, slowing the progress of both himself and Rex. Time seemed to stand still, then he heard the screech of brakes. Johnny stood unmoving for a moment, as though paralysed by shock, but from the corner of his eye he saw that the second van had braked to a halt also. Immediately all of the workmen that had been digging the pavement swarmed around the two vehicles, their tools suddenly dropped and with pistols in hand.

There were screams and shouts, and what Johnny hoped were warning shots, as the rebels held up the police convoy. But Johnny's instructions on what to do now had been crystal clear. He sprinted away with the dog, resisting the temptation to look back, and making sure not to show his face. He quickly mounted the steps leading up to Royal Canal Bank, then ran into the maze of streets that surrounded the City Basin. Rounding the corner into Fontenoy Street, he passed the dog's lead to a waiting man who instantly headed off with Rex in the opposite direction. Johnny whipped off his cap and gabardine overcoat, then jumped into the back of a waiting car that pulled off at once.

In the distance he heard more shots, then the car accelerated further. Johnny's heart felt like it would explode. He sat back in the seat, mouthing a silent prayer, and hoping fervently that their rescue had succeeded.

CHAPTER EIGHT

Normally Stella loved roast chicken, but tonight she ate mechanically, her mind elsewhere as she had dinner with her father in the dining room of the Mill Hotel. She wished that things could stay on an even keel, but lately her own life had been a series of dramatic ups and downs. The saddest thing was Granddad being in a coma, but the devastation of Balbriggan by the Tans and Auxies was still upsetting.

She tried to stay optimistic, the way Alice did, and now she made herself do the exercise where she concentrated on positive developments. She reminded herself that she had saved Johnny's life on the night of the fires, and she recalled with satisfaction that first one hundred women had been admitted to Oxford University, in what she thought was a long overdue piece of progress.

There was also the fact that her father had reluctantly given her permission to attend the fund-raising sports day in Lusk for the victims of the Sack of Balbriggan, as the night of mayhem was now being called.

Stella had argued that she didn't want to be the only girl in her class who wasn't going, and Dad had given in. She knew that her father suspected the event might turn into an outlet for anti-government protest, and she was grateful that he was willing to overlook that, so that she wouldn't be out on a limb with her classmates.

She looked at him now across the table. He appeared smart in a well-cut tweed suit, but Stella thought he looked tired. 'Are you run ragged at Baldonnel, Dad?' she asked.

'Do I look that worn out?' he asked.

'Just a little tired, maybe.'

'It's been fairly hectic,' he conceded.

'What's making it so busy?'

'Well, for one thing the RAF's being asked to provide a mail service.'

'What, delivering letters?'

'And plans and written orders. It's dangerous to send them by road to barracks in rebel territory. So now we deliver them by air.'

'I suppose that makes sense,' said Stella.

'And we're doing more reconnaissance, for rebel training camps and arms dumps.'

'Right.'

'But it's a constant battle of wits.'

'Why, what are the rebels doing?' asked Stella, her curiosity piqued.

'Well, when we organised dropping circles – so our pilots would know where to drop messages – the rebels set up phoney ones. To trick us into dropping our messages into their hands.'

Stella thought that was clever. She didn't want to be disloyal, however, so she didn't say so. 'Really?' she answered. 'And how did you get around that?'

'Now we only drop if they have a recognised identity sign at the dropping circle.'

'It's very cat and mouse, isn't it?' said Stella.

'Absolutely. They carry out operations at night, so we bring in a curfew. They still operate under cover of darkness, so we use searchlights. One side gets the upper hand, the other side makes a counter-move.'

Stella wanted to ask where it would all end, but something held her back. If Dad admitted that the rebels would eventually win she would be glad for Johnny and for the Irish people, but sad for her father. But if the British authorities stamped out the independence movement, Johnny would be heart-broken. And the wishes of the majority of Irish voters for either independence or Home Rule would have been ignored.

Before Stella could grapple further with her thoughts, Mrs Goodman approached their table.

'Good evening, Wing Commander,' she said warmly. 'Everything all right?'

'Fine, thank you, Mrs Goodman, delicious food.'

'How are you, Stella?'

'Very well, thanks.'

'Looking forward to your trip to the museum?'

Before Stella could respond her father looked at her quizzically. 'I thought you were going to visit the National Gallery?'

Stella tried to hide her surprise. In planning their trip to find Johnny in Dublin they had said that they would claim to be visiting the museum or the gallery. Now, though, Stella realised that they had been sloppy in not making sure to have their story straight.

'I thought it was the gallery,' she answered, seeking to keep her tone casual, 'but maybe I got it wrong.'

'Alice seemed quite definite,' said Mrs Goodman.

'Then it must be my mistake,' said Stella quickly. She avoided her father's eyes, knowing it would be harder to sustain a lie if he was looking at her. *But was he already suspicious?*

'Either way,' said Mrs Goodman, 'it's no harm for young ladies to broaden their education. Wouldn't you agree, Commander?'

Stella found herself holding her breath as she finally turned to face her father. If he thought something suspicious was going on, now was his chance to ask awkward questions.

He looked at Mrs Goodman, then answered politely. 'I couldn't agree more,' he said, 'very educational.'

Stella made a conscious effort not to show her relief. But she had given herself a needless fright, and she promised herself that she wouldn't do it again. If she was going to re-establish contact with Johnny – and she really wanted to – then she would need to be much more careful.

'Hey, Dunner, want to celebrate your first full pay packet? We're going round to the shop.'

Johnny was touched that the other telegraph boys were making him welcome and he hesitated on his way to the bicycle shed. It was Friday evening, and they had all just received their pay packets from Mr Williams in the telegraph office. Williams had kept up the front of being strict with Johnny in public, but privately he had been encouraging. He had also skilfully arranged Johnny's work so as to allow him time to track whichever British agents Michael Collins's intelligence officers were investigating.

Johnny in turn had slotted in easily at the job, getting along well with his fellow workers. Now, though, he faced a quandary. Part of him wanted to be one of the lads, treating himself at the shop after a hard week's work. And he really liked Nedser, the boy who had invited him to the shops. But it was dangerous to get too friendly with anyone while carrying out his mission, and this evening he had a reason to head straight home.

'Thanks, lads, but I've something on. Maybe next week,' said Johnny, then he quickly waved farewell and headed off before anyone could question him.

He mounted his bicycle and began cycling home, eager to get to Gardiner Place. It was three days now since the rescue of Mr O'Shea, and Johnny was still thrilled by the daring of what they had done. Two policeman and one of the volunteers had been wounded, but the element of surprise and the painstaking planning had paid off, and the mission had been a resounding success. Johnny had found out later that O'Shea had been whisked away in another car, after which he had lain low for the last three days.

Mrs Hanlon had praised Johnny for his part in the rescue, and before he had left for work this morning she had said that O'Shea wanted to see Johnny in person. It was rare for Mrs Hanlon to give more details than necessary, so Johnny took it as a big compliment when she revealed that O'Shea would be in Gardiner Place this evening.

He cycled on, the crisp October air getting colder with the setting of the sun. Johnny rode across the broad expanse of Sackville Street, dodging the clanking trams that criss-crossed the busy city centre. He cut up through Marlborough Street, avoiding the strong-smelling dung deposited on the cobbled street by the horse-drawn traffic that was gradually being replaced by motor cars, vans and trucks.

But if progress was being made regarding transport, there was still a long way to go when it came to housing the citizens of Dublin. Now that he was more familiar with the city from his telegram deliveries, Johnny was horrified by the contrast between the grinding poverty of the tenements and the affluence of suburbs like Rathgar and Rathmines.

He turned into Great Britain Street, passing a foul-smelling tenement. On its steps some gaunt-faced children were playing listlessly. They were barefoot despite the cold, and it underlined for Johnny the pressing need for the new Ireland for which he was fighting.

The sight of the children dampened his mood, and he hoped that their father might bring home a Friday pay packet to brighten their lives, even temporarily.

Thinking of Friday night, his mind drifted to Balbriggan. He recalled how Friday night used to be his favourite time of the week, when he attended band practice with his friends. Although he was a better musician than Alice or Stella, at band practice everyone was treated as an equal by the bandmaster, Mr Tardelli, and Johnny loved that relaxed, all-in-it-together atmosphere. He recalled a vision of Alice, pretending to be heart-broken after playing a wrong note in '*Funiculi, Funicula*' and he felt a sudden welling of affection for his friends. He missed the banter with the band members, and Mr Tardelli's jokes and riddles, but most of all he missed Alice and Stella. He hoped they were well, and he felt bad at having lied to them in the postcards. His orders had been clear, however, and all he could do now was hope to renew their friendship after his mission was over.

Approaching the incline of Hill Street, Johnny rose in the saddle and pedalled hard, eager now to get home as soon as possible. He wondered what Mr O'Shea would look like, and if he bore any marks of abuse from being questioned during his time in custody. Well, he would know soon enough, he thought as he reached the junction of Hill Street and Gardiner Place. He rode around to the rear of Hanlon's and locked his bicycle in the yard. He entered by the back door and encountered Bridget, the middle-aged cook.

'Ah, Johnny. Mrs H is expecting you. She said to go up.'

'Thanks, Bridget,' he said, then he took the stairs two at a time to the first floor where the owner had her private rooms. Johnny had never been inside Mrs Hanlon's quarters before and he felt slightly nervous as he knocked on the door.

He waited expectantly, then the door opened, and Mrs Hanlon stood before him, her piercing blue eyes seeming to weigh him up.

'Johnny,' she said. 'You made good time. Come in.'

Johnny entered the living room, which was furnished much more expensively than the downstairs parlour. He barely had time to notice the good taste of the décor when Mr O'Shea rose from an armchair before the fire.

'Johnny, good to see you again!' he said, offering his hand.

'Good to see you too, Mr O,' answered Johnny as they shook hands warmly.

He noticed that O'Shea looked tired, and although clean shaven and well dressed, he didn't look as dapper as when he had stayed at the Mill Hotel as a traveller for Glentoran Whiskey. On the other hand he showed no marks that suggested being beaten up during his weeks of captivity, and Johnny was relieved.

'Let's sit at the fire,' suggested Mrs Hanlon. 'Bridget will serve some food after we chat.'

'Great,' said Johnny, tired after a busy day and happy to take the weight off his feet in a comfortable armchair.

They all settled themselves, then O'Shea spoke, his tone serious.

'I just want to say, Johnny, I'm grateful for your help in springing me. Very grateful.'

'You're welcome. But I just played a small part.'

'No, son, you played a key part, and I'm in your debt.'

'Thanks,' said Johnny. 'Though if it comes to that, I'm in your debt too.'

'How's that?'

'When you were arrested you never told them about me. I'm sure…I'm sure they tried to make you name names.'

A hard look came into Mr O'Shea's eyes and he spoke flatly. 'They did. But they were never, ever going to hear your name from me.'

'Thanks.'

'And now I hear you're doing good work again,' said O'Shea, his tone brightening.

'I'm happy to help any way I can.'

'I know that, Johnny. And to show it works both ways, I've been spoken to by the Boss. About the orphanage.'

Johnny realised that his request to Michael Collins hadn't been dismissed and he felt a surge of excitement. 'Really?'

'Maybe next week you and I could pay a visit to St Mary's. See can we get some answers. What do you think?'

'That would be great. The only thing is….the brothers are very…they mightn't want to co-operate.'

'We'll see about that.'

The firm way O'Shea said it gave Johnny hope. 'You really think we could get some information?'

'Leave the brothers to me. Will we say Tuesday evening?'

'Yes. Yes, absolutely!'

'OK, Tuesday it is so.'

Johnny could hardly believe it. After all these years maybe he could finally find out about his family. Mrs Hanlon and O'Shea began discussing the best way to travel to St Mary's Orphanage, but Johnny barely listened, his mind racing as he wished away the hours till Tuesday night.

CHAPTER NINE

'I've bad news!' said Alice, slipping onto a chair opposite Stella, as her friend had breakfast in the dining room of the Mill.

'What?' asked Stella, pushing aside her teacup.

'I can't go to Dublin. It's *so* annoying!'

It was Saturday morning, and the girls had planned to take an early train to the city in their quest to make contact with Johnny.

'What's happened?'

Alice tried to dampen her frustration and she spoke more calmly. 'It's my own fault. I pushed Mam to get involved in tomorrow's Sports Day. And now she's agreed to doing the catering, and I have to help.'

'I thought she didn't want to get involved.'

'She didn't. But I told her we're seen as too pro-British, and besides, the Sports Day is to help the people of Balbriggan, so we should play our part.'

'Right.'

'And now Mam, being Mam, wants to do it properly – first class catering.'

'Fair enough.'

'Not fair enough, Stella! I'll be stuck here helping.'

'Did you try to get out of it?'

'Yes, but I can't protest too much without sounding suspicious. She'll just say to visit the museum another Saturday.'

'I suppose we could put it off for a week,' said Stella.

'Or you could still go.'

'On my own?'

'Why not? We want to know what's going on with Johnny.'

'Well, yes, but—'

'God knows what could happen in another week, Stella. The sooner we find him the better.' Alice could see that her friend was torn. 'Look,' she said persuasively. 'You've told your dad that you're going to Dublin with me and Bernie Dowling, right?'

'Yes, I said we're doing a class project.'

'So take the chance while you have it. Maybe next week he'll want you to spend the day with him, or there'll be some other problem.'

Still Stella hesitated, and Alice felt a little guilty. 'I'm sorry,' she said, 'I don't mean to bully you. If you want to leave it, we can both go another time.'

To her surprise, Stella shook her head. 'No, you're right, we shouldn't put this off. I know my way around Dublin, there's no excuse. I'll do it.'

'Sure?'

'Yes.'

Alice felt a surge of affection and she reached out and squeezed her friend's arm. 'Well done, Stells, you're a gem!'

* * *

The policeman walked towards Stella, his eyes seeming to bore into her. Loitering in the street near the entrance to the telegraph office on a day that was cloudy and cold had made her feel conspicuous, and now the constable drew nearer, pounding out his beat.

Stella wanted to run away but she resisted the impulse. *Don't panic*, she told herself. *What he sees is a well-dressed girl who appears to be standing in the street for no apparent reason. So create a reason.*

Moving before she fully knew what she was doing, Stella took the initiative and walked towards the constable. 'Excuse me, sir,' she said politely, aware that her accent and delivery would stamp her as respectable in his eyes. 'Could you tell me, please, where the terminus is for the Sandymount tram?'

Stella could tell that the policeman was appraising her and she smiled. 'I've to meet my friend off the tram,' she added.

'It runs from the Pillar, Miss, just around the corner.'

'Thank you.'

Stella headed off as though making for Nelson's Pillar. Once out of sight of the constable, however, she paused and stepped into a busy cake shop. She stood as though choosing from the array of confectionery, but in fact she watched the progress of the patrolling policeman. As soon as he was gone from sight Stella left the shop and made her way back towards the telegraph office.

It was lunchtime now, and she was hoping to intercept Johnny. She reasoned that after a morning of delivering telegrams he would return to base to have his lunch. *Unless he had a picnic lunch wherever his deliveries took him.* No, she decided, she had to remain positive.

She had already got a discouraging response when she had gone to the reception desk at the telegraph office. She had decided to try the direct approach and had asked if she could speak with a staff member called Johnny Dunne. Instead the supervisor, a Mr Williams, had come to reception and spoken discreetly to her, out of earshot of the receptionist.

'I'm told you were making enquiries,' he said.

'Yes, I want to contact Johnny Dunne. Does he work from this office?'

Stella sensed a wariness about the supervisor, even though he kept his tone neutral.

'May I ask what this is about?' said Williams.

'He's a friend I've lost contact with,' answered Stella, deciding to keep her story as near as possible to the truth. 'A girl I know saw him on a telegraph bicycle, so I thought I'd come here.'

'I see.'

'So, does Johnny work from this office?'

'I'm sorry,' said Mr Williams. 'But I can't give out details regarding staff.'

'I'm not asking for private details. I just want to know if he's based here. I don't want to disturb him during working hours, I only want a word during his lunch break, or even after work.'

'I'm sorry, Miss, but I have to respect staff privacy. I'm afraid we can't have members of the public coming in and seeking out staff.'

'I understand that. All I'm asking is if this is his place of work?'

'And all I can say, is that I have to respect staff privacy. So, if there's nothing else…'

Stella realised that she wasn't going to get anywhere, and if this man was Johnny's boss she didn't want to get her friend into trouble.

'Very well. Thank you anyway,' she said. 'Good day.'

'Good day, Miss.'

That had been about an hour previously, and Stella had walked away as though defeated. After a moment, though, she had doubled back, and since then she had casually strolled back and forth along the busy street. Now she took up her position again. But her trip to Dublin was starting to feel like a wild goose chase. Supposing Esther Moore was mistaken? Supposing she had simply seen a boy who looked like Johnny?

And then, suddenly, Stella saw him. There had been no mistake. Coming around the corner, dressed in his post office uniform, Johnny cycled into view.

Stella moved quickly, wanting to intercept him before he reached the telegraph office. She crossed the road, and stood on the pavement where he couldn't miss her. Johnny looked up, then quickly braked. His shock was obvious, and Stella hoped that he wouldn't be angry that she had tracked him down. But then again, he had lied to her. So if anyone was entitled to be angry, surely it was her. Well, it would be clear soon enough, she thought.

'Stella!' he said, dismounting from the bicycle, the surprise still visible on his face.

'Hello, Johnny,' she said. 'I think…I think we need to talk.'

The midday sun suddenly emerged from the clouds, bathing Sackville Street with autumn sunshine. Johnny, however, was oblivious to his surroundings as he sat with Stella on one of the seats at the base of the O'Connell Monument. They had bought milk and buns from a street stall and were having a picnic lunch before Johnny returned to work.

All around them the bustling life of the city went on, with horse-drawn carts clattering down the quays while trams, cars, and bicycles travelled up and down Sackville street. Johnny drank his milk, still a little in shock that Stella had come to Dublin and tracked him down.

She turned to him now, her bun uneaten and a serious look on her face.

'I need to ask you something, Johnny,' she said.

'I think I know what it is.'

'Why…why did you lie to me and Alice in the postcards?'

Johnny found it hard to hold her gaze, but he forced himself not to look away. 'I had to,' he said.

'Why's that?'

'I can't tell you.'

'You can't, or you won't?'

'I can't. It's…it's complicated.'

'Is it? I thought it was straight-forward. I thought we were friends.'

'We are. But…' Johnny struggled to find the right words, and Stella drew closer.

'Why is there a "but" if we're the kind of friends I thought we were?' she said softly.

Johnny felt a stab of guilt. His emotions had been in a whirl since encountering Stella – shock at her sudden appearance, pleasure at seeing her again, frustration that his mission called for strict secrecy. And now he felt really bad on being reminded of how good a friend Stella had been. First she had saved his life when he was trapped in the burning building, and now she had come all the way to Dublin to see him. He couldn't just palm her off, no matter what Mrs Hanlon had said about security.

'There were two reasons I lied,' he said reluctantly.

'Yes?'

'The first is that I'm involved in the struggle again, and they insisted nobody knows.'

Johnny could see that Stella wasn't happy with this news, but he carried on. 'The second reason is that if things go wrong, I don't want to drag you and Alice into it.'

'How would we be dragged into it?'

'If we exchanged letters, they'd see your address. I didn't want to cause problems for either of you if I got arrested. And the Mill is

Mrs Goodman's livelihood. I don't want the Tans burning it down 'cause the Goodmans are linked to a rebel.'

Stella looked thoughtful, and Johnny reached out and touched her arm.

'I'm really sorry for lying to you. But I had no choice.'

'It's OK, Johnny. I understand. But…have you not done enough for the cause? If you keep on taking risks, sooner or later…' Stella shook her head. 'I don't even want to think of what might happen.'

'It won't be forever. But for the next couple of months I have a mission. It's important.'

'Why does it have to be you doing it?'

'I want things to change, Stella, I've a duty to play my part.'

'A duty? You're only fourteen!'

'My age has nothing to do with it. I've a duty, just like your Dad has a duty. You mightn't like what he's doing either, but he still has to do it.'

'That's different.'

'How is it different?'

'One, he's an adult. And two, he's in the Air Force. He's in uniform, Johnny, he's not spying!'

'You think what the RAF does is more noble than spying?'

'I didn't say that.'

'The RAF buzzed civilians outside Mountjoy Jail to disperse them. They're hunting our men in the hills, they're searching for arms dumps. Your Dad does all that because it's his duty. And I'm doing what I do because that's *my* duty. You can't ask me not to do it, Stella. If I walked away now I...I wouldn't be me.'

There was a long pause, then Stella nodded. 'All right, Johnny. All right.'

He looked at her, not knowing where that left him. 'So, can we...'

'What?'

'Can we put all this aside, and be friends again when it's over?'

He waited anxiously for her answer, and when she spoke her voice sounded emotional. 'We don't have to wait till it's over. We're friends now and we'll be friends then too. I know you can't tell me what you're up to, but please, just promise you won't be reckless. That you won't take more risks than you have to.'

Johnny felt hugely relieved by her reply. 'OK,' he said with a crooked grin. 'I don't have a death wish. I promise I'll be careful. All right?'

For the first time Stella gave a weak smile. 'All right.'

'So enough about me,' said Johnny, sipping from his milk and taking a bite from his bun. 'Tell me your news, what's happening in Balbriggan?'

'They're planning to rebuild the burnt-down buildings. There's a big fund raiser at a sports day tomorrow.'

'Brilliant. And how's Mr Tardelli?'

'He's well. Actually, he was talking about you.'

'Really?'

'We're learning this new song – "They Didn't Believe Me."'

'Great tune.'

'You know it?'

'Yes.'

'Anyway, he was saying "I wish Johnny was here." He said a clarinet part would be perfect in the song.'

'Good ol' Mr T!' said Johnny.

'Yes…'

For a moment Stella was silent, and Johnny looked at her enquiringly.

'What is it?' he asked softly

'It's … it's just my own news isn't so good.'

'Oh? What's wrong?'

'It's Granddad. He's slipped into a coma.'

'Oh, Stella. I'm really sorry. Is there…is there any chance he'll come out of it?'

Stella shook her head. 'No, he…he hasn't got long.'

'I don't know what to say. I'm…I'm just so sorry.'

'Thanks, Johnny. It's been coming for a while, but it was still horrible when Dad told me.'

'Of course. I wish I'd been around to…well, I don't know what I could have done, but just to be there.'

'You'd have been there if you could.'

'Absolutely.'

'I know. I never doubted that for a second.'

Johnny wanted to respond, but he felt a lump in his throat.

'And Alice…she's been great,' said Stella.

'Yes, she's dead loyal. When things are tough it's good to have someone to count on.'

'You, me and Alice – I want us always to be pals,' said Stella solemnly. 'No matter what else happens.'

'I want that too,' said Johnny. But somehow words didn't seem to be enough, and he held out his hand. 'Let's shake on it.'

Stella reached out and shook his hand, and Johnny knew, instinctively, that this was a promise never to be broken.

PART TWO

REVELATIONS

CHAPTER TEN

'How did Mr Tardelli ever get a job in this school?' asked Alice, as she and Stella left the music room and headed down the corridor for the mid-morning break.

'How do you mean?'

'The other teachers are so straight-laced. How did Mr T slip through the net?'

'They're not *all* straight-laced,' said Stella.

'Most of them are. It's a miracle the nuns hired Mr Tardelli.'

'Yes and no,' answered Stella. 'He's colourful, but he's a great musician, and a good teacher, and he's a Catholic. You can see why the nuns would like him.'

'Maybe Sister Mary took a shine to him!'

'Alice! You can't say that – she's a nun!'

'Even so. I mean, I know he's ancient – he must be about forty if he's a day – but he's still kind of good looking.'

'Well, yes…'

'Maybe Sister Mary likes men with sallow skin and dark hair!'

Stella looked slightly shocked, but she laughed. 'Why don't you ask her?'

'Can you imagine? Please, Sister, what is it you find irresistible in a man?!'

Stella laughed again, then they reached the end of the corridor and stepped out the door leading to the school yard. The October air was cool, but there was hazy sunshine that gave a shimmer to the nearby waters of the Irish Sea. Despite the cries of the school yard, the atmosphere felt still, with barely a hint of a breeze troubling the surface of the water.

'I love when the sea looks really calm,' said Stella.

'Yeah.' Alice paused, then spoke seriously. 'If only everything was as calm….'

Stella nodded, and there was no need for the friends to elaborate on what it was that worried them. Yesterday's Sports Day had been a success, with badly needed money raised for the Balbriggan fund, yet despite the sports, and pony racing, and Irish dancing, Alice's enjoyment of the event had been dampened by Stella's report of her meeting in Dublin with Johnny.

'I wish there was some way we could protect Johnny,' said Alice after a moment.

'He swore me to secrecy, we can't tell anyone.'

'I know.'

'All we can do is pray that whatever he's at, he comes through safely.'

'Praying is all very well,' said Alice. 'But I'd love to be able to *do* something.'

'Like what? We've wracked out brains.'

'Maybe we should wrack them a bit more. If something happens to him, while we do nothing, we'll never forgive ourselves.'

Her friend went to respond, but Alice held up a hand to cut her short. 'You could be right, Stella. Maybe there's nothing we can do. But maybe, just maybe, there is. Let's not stop trying to figure out what that might be. OK?'

'OK,' said Stella. 'OK.'

Johnny tried to appear calm as he drove with Mr O'Shea towards St Mary's orphanage. He sat in the passenger seat of the car, beside the former commercial traveller, who glanced inquiringly at Johnny as he drove through the early evening traffic.

'You followed Lieutenant Peel yesterday, didn't you?'

'Yes.'

'He's dangerous. He was posted here from Russia. Be really, really careful there, Johnny.'

'Don't worry, Mr O, I'm on full alert when I trail any of them.'

'Good. Because you're not dealing with the army or the regular police here. These men are experienced intelligence agents – they're ruthless.'

'Right.' Johnny swallowed hard, remembering yesterday and the fright he had received when Lieutenant Peel had suddenly turned around while Johnny had been following him down North Earl Street. The Englishman had done it smoothly, as though he had suddenly remembered something that required him to alter course. But Johnny suspected that it was the move of a trained agent who wanted to see if anyone was tailing him. Johnny's heart had pounded in this chest at the time, but he had managed to walk casually past the intelligence officer while sorting through a bunch of telegrams. *No need to worry O'Shea by telling him about the incident now*, thought Johnny, who had already resolved to be careful in the extreme if he had to follow Lieutenant Peel again.

'So, this Brother Kenny at the orphanage,' said O'Shea, breaking Johnny's reverie. 'You don't have to be afraid of him anymore. Just let me handle him.'

'OK.'

In truth Johnny *was* still afraid of Brother Kenny, but looking across at Mr O'Shea, he felt reassured. Since his escape from prison O'Shea had been working full time for the rebels, and with his smartly cut suit and driving a gleaming – if borrowed – motor car, he exuded the confident air of a successful businessman. Johnny knew though that he could be decisive and ruthless when necessary.

'Right then,' said O'Shea, 'let's see if we can get some answers for you.'

Johnny steeled himself, determined to look unconcerned. They were in the reception area in St Mary's now, but the moment O'Shea had turned into the avenue leading to the orphanage Johnny had felt anxious. All the old, horrible memories of being beaten, and hungry and cold had flooded back. He had had to remind himself that he was no longer at the mercy of the brothers, and that he had an ally in Mr O'Shea who was tougher and more fearless than anyone they were likely to encounter in St Mary's. It had been a pleasant surprise to Johnny when Mrs Hanlon and Mr O'Shea had been so sympathetic about his suffering in the orphanage – lots of people weren't bothered about the welfare of orphans – and he put their attitude down to the idealism that made them also want a better Ireland.

The weak evening sun was starting to set now, and Johnny knew that the boys would be eating in the refectory, which accounted for the fact that he hadn't seen any of the orphans as they had entered the building. Johnny had followed O'Shea's instructions to wear his best clothes, and despite his anxiety, he still felt much more assured than when he had been a helpless inmate here, dressed in drab, ill-fitting hand-me-downs.

O'Shea confidently rang the bell on the desk, and Johnny recognised Mr Roche, the caretaker who came in answer. If the man recognised Johnny he gave no indication, but taking in O'Shea's expensive clothes, he spoke deferentially.

'Can I help you, sir?

'Yes, I'd like to speak to Brother Kenny, please.'

'Can I say who it is, sir?'

'Mr Smith. Tell him it's a matter of urgency, please.'

'Very good, sir.'

The caretaker went through a door behind the reception desk, and O'Shea turned and winked. Johnny forced himself to smile in return, but his mouth went dry when Brother Kenny strode in to reception a moment later.

Johnny was standing a little to the side so the brother didn't notice him, his attention directed to O'Shea.

'You wished to see me?' said Kenny.

Johnny was interested to see that the brother's tone was polite, and he realised that he was responding to O'Shea's smart appearance.

'Yes,' answered O'Shea. 'I'd like to make a donation to St Mary's.'

'How very kind.'

'Well, my nephew here, Johnny, is a former pupil.'

Kenny turned around, and Johnny saw the shock in his eyes. He recovered quickly though and gave a phoney smile. 'Yes indeed, I remember Johnny. A very talented musician.'

Johnny swallowed hard, his blood boiling. In all his years in the orphanage Kenny had never once acknowledged his talent. He felt like screaming at his former tormentor, of reminding him of the beatings and his needless cruelty, but instead he stared Kenny in the eye, refusing to smile back.

'Could we pop into your office, perhaps, to work out a few details?' suggested O'Shea.

'Certainly. This way, please.'

Kenny ushered them in through the door, and the smell of the waxed corridor they entered brought back memories to Johnny of orphans on their knees, polishing its surface as if their lives depended on it.

They came to an office, which Kenny unlocked, then the brother seated himself behind a large mahogany desk, indicating for Johnny and O'Shea to sit opposite him.

'So, you very kindly wished to support St Mary's? Mr Smith, isn't it?'

'That's right,' answered O'Shea, reaching forward and placing a ten-shilling note on the desk. 'There you are.'

Johnny saw the confusion on Kenny's face.

'That's your donation?'

'Have you a problem with that?' asked O'Shea.

'I thought…'

'It's just a small gesture,' said O'Shea, cutting the brother off. 'To compensate for disturbing your dinner, and perhaps to give the boys a little treat. God knows they could do with it from what Johnny has told me.'

Kenny's face darkened, but before he could respond O'Shea continued, his tone relaxed and almost friendly. 'And talking of Johnny, I'd like you to oblige me by consulting your records. Johnny wishes to know who his parents were.'

'Does he indeed?' said Kenny, all pretence at goodwill gone from his voice.

'He's entitled to know who his family are.'

'You said you're his uncle. Surely then he knows who his family are.'

'Not an uncle by blood or by marriage. But I'm like an uncle. And now he wants to know his background. It's not a lot to ask.'

'It *is* a lot to ask. It's confidential information. He was fed, clothed and educated at St Mary's. We owe him nothing more than that.'

'That's where we differ,' answered O'Shea, his tone hardening. 'I'd say he was beaten, starved and abused in St Mary's. I'd say you owe him an abject apology.'

'How dare you?'

'But we're not demanding an apology,' said O'Shea, ignoring the brother's anger. 'We'll settle for the information on his family.'

'That's not possible. Now I'd like you to leave.'

'We'll be happy to leave. But not without the information.'

'I'm afraid you don't understand. I'm not obliged to tell you anything.'

'Well, you're right about one thing. You're right to be afraid.'

Johnny had been fascinated by how O'Shea was handling Kenny, and now he saw the brother's face begin to flush with anger.

'Are you…are you threatening me?'

O'Shea didn't answer, but instead unbuttoned the jacket of his suit, reached into the inside pocket, and took out a Webley revolver. He placed the weapon on the edge of the desk, then looked Kenny in the eye.

'I'm politely asking, one more time,' said O'Shea.

Johnny couldn't help but enjoy the shock on the brother's face.

'You can't…you can't come in here and threaten me!' he spluttered.

'No?'

'How dare you think that—'

'How dare I? Well, that's easy. I've spent the last two years fighting the RIC, the British Army, the Black and Tans and the Auxies. Putting manners on a bully of a Christian Brother is small potatoes.'

'I don't have to listen to this,' said O'Shea, rising behind the desk.

'Actually, you do,' said O'Shea, taking up the gun and aiming it. 'But if you think I'm bluffing, try walking out the door. I promise you, it'll be the last time you walk anywhere. Your choice.'

There was a long pause, and Johnny found himself holding his breath. Would O'Shea really shoot if Brother Kenny called his bluff? For a moment nobody said anything, and no one moved. Then Kenny breathed out angrily and sat down again.

'Good,' said O'Shea. 'Now that we know I'm serious, we can put this away.' He slipped the pistol back into his jacket pocket. 'All right, Johnny, if you wouldn't mind opening the door, Brother Kenny will lead us to the records office.'

The last rays of the evening sun shone in through the window, the temperature dropping and the wind blowing against the window pane. The records office felt cold and musty, but Johnny's sense of numbness had little to do with the weather. He stared at his birth cert, and the St Mary's records, his head swirling as he tried to process what he had learnt. Johnny Dunne, born May 13th 1906 to Norah Dunne, chemist's assistant, and Josef Lazlo, musician. It certainly explained where his musical talent came from, but who was Josef Lazlo and how had he ended up in Ireland? Why did he not have his father's surname? And why had Josef Lazlo and Norah Dunne placed him in an orphanage? He knew that if a woman who was unmarried had a baby it was often taken for adoption, and he had long since had to accept that that was probably what had happened in his own case. But Norah Dunne had an address in Athlone. Could her family not have taken her in, and spared Johnny the horrors of St Mary's? Or maybe she had died in childbirth. There were so many unanswered questions. But knowing who his parents were meant he now had a starting point for more enquiries.

'Ready to go, Johnny?' said O'Shea. 'I've jotted down all the details for you.'

'OK.'

'Before we leave though, you and I have a bit of business,' said O'Shea, turning to Brother Kenny. 'Beating the last two boys into the shower each time, and then making a laugh of it? That's a pretty sick joke, mister. You need to stop that.'

Johnny saw the anger flaring up in Kenny's eyes. 'Who the hell do you think you are!' he snapped at O'Shea. 'You got what you came for. Quit while you're ahead, if you know what's good for you.'

'You're the one who needs to learn what's good for you,' said

O'Shea, then he suddenly pivoted and punched Kenny in the stomach.

The brother doubled over and sank, gasping, to his knees. O'Shea grabbed him by the lapels and dragged him up until their faces were just inches apart. 'If you do that beating-at-the shower routine to another child, it won't be just a punch you get. Johnny is still in touch with boys here, and he'll hear about it if you don't stop.'

Johnny was taken aback by O'Shea's claim – he hadn't been in touch with anyone in St Mary's since the day he had left – but then Kenny wasn't to know that.

'If Johnny hears that you haven't stopped,' continued O'Shea, 'I'll be paying you a visit in the middle of the night. And the thump you just got, that will be like a caress compared to what I'll give you if I've to come back here. Understood?'

Johnny looked at his old tormentor, fascinated to see that the man who had frightened so many boys was now frightened himself. No longer a figure of terror, Johnny now saw him for what he was, an overweight, middle-aged man with bad breath and dandruff on his collar.

'I said is that understood?' insisted O'Shea.

'Yes,' gasped Kenny, 'yes, it is.'

'Good.' O'Shea released the other man, then turned to Johnny. 'I think we're finished here. Unless there's anything you want to say to Brother Kenny.'

'I'll never, ever, have anything to say to Brother Kenny,' Johnny answered, looking at him with disdain.

'In that case let's get out of here.'

'Yeah, let's,' said Johnny, then he turned his back on Kenny and walked briskly out the door.

CHAPTER ELEVEN

'If Finland can be independent, why can't Ireland?'

It was a good question, and Stella didn't have a ready answer. She was in the junior chess club with Alice, and Padraig Egan, the one boy in the club that she had never liked, had asked her the question aggressively.

Finland had just won independence from Russia, and Stella had been coming to the view that perhaps Ireland should be independent of Britain. But she didn't want to be publicly disloyal to her father, and she sensed that Padraig had posed the question to put her on the spot.

They were in a break between games, and she could see that the other club members were watching her, curious to see how she would respond.

'Maybe Ireland can be independent in time,' she answered.

'Not if people like your father have their way,' said Padraig.

'My father just does his duty,' answered Stella, 'he doesn't get to decide on Home Rule or Independence.'

'But he's English, so even if he did get to decide, he'd probably want to keep us down.'

'Don't talk rubbish, Padraig,' said Alice.

Stella felt a surge of affection for her; it was typical of Alice to defend a friend.

'Who's talking rubbish?' demanded Padraig.

'You are. You've never even met Stella's father, have you?'

'No, but—'

'Well I have. And he's not the sort to want to put anyone down. So cut it out.'

Padraig glanced around, seeking support, but Stella was pleased to see that the club members seemed to have been swayed by Alice.

'Leave it, Padraig,' said one of the other boys.

'Or better still, do your fighting on the chess board,' said Alice. 'I'll take you on, and if you beat me I'll buy you an ice cream – and call you "your majesty"!'

There was cheering and laughter from the other members, and even Padraig gave a wry grin. 'You're on!' he said.

Stella watched them setting up the chess board. She thought how lucky she was to have a friend like Alice. She thought too that it was clever of Alice to lighten the mood with humour, having made her point with Padraig. And what would Padraig Egan think if he knew that her other friend, Johnny Dunne, whose life she had saved, was actively engaged in the war of independence?

Life was complicated, what with defending Dad on one hand, yet deceiving him regarding her involvement with Johnny, and her growing sympathy for his cause. She was about to take a seat and watch Alice's match, when Mr Rooney, the local chess master and founder of the club, entered the room.

'Stella Radcliffe,' he called.

'Yes,' said Stella, rising from her seat.

'Could we talk in private, please?'

'Eh...yes,' answered Stella, wondering why on earth Mr Rooney needed to speak to her in private. 'I'll be back to cheer you on,' she said to Alice, then she crossed to Mr Rooney.

He looked serious, and Stella felt a twinge of unease. But she had done nothing wrong, and she told herself not to be so fretful. Stepping out onto the landing, she saw her father, and she stopped dead, knowing that something important must have happened for him to interrupt her chess club.

'Dad,' she said. 'What's wrong?'

He looked pained, and even as she asked the question, in her heart she knew the answer.

'It's...it's Granddad,' her father said. 'I'm afraid...I'm afraid he's gone.'

Although Stella had known that this moment was coming, the shock hit her hard, and she felt her throat constricting and her eyes welling up.

Suddenly Padraig Egan, and the war, and even Johnny Dunne were banished from her mind, as she grappled with the reality of never seeing her beloved Granddad again.

'I'm so sorry, darling,' said her father, his voice shaky.

Stella just nodded, then she ran to him, and sobbing softly, buried herself in his arms.

Alice watched anxiously as Johnny approached her. She was seated at the base of the O'Connell monument, where Stella had talked with Johnny the previous week. Now he nipped between the lunchtime traffic that trundled up and down the broad expanse of Sackville Street, and Alice swallowed nervously as he drew near. She knew that she was breaking Johnny's rule about not meeting. But she had to see him, and she had lied to Mam about another trip to Dublin with school friends, taken the morning train, and left a note for Johnny at the telegraph office asking him to meet her.

'Alice,' he said, sitting beside her. 'This isn't a good idea.'

Despite knowing that Johnny wasn't meant to meet anyone while on his mission, she felt disappointed. She realised that her feelings must have shown, for Johnny reached out and touched her arm.

'It's not that I don't want to see you. I really do. But it's risky for you to be linked to me.'

'I know,' answered Alice, 'but I had to meet you. I've news you should hear in person. I didn't want to just send a letter.'

Johnny looked at her seriously. All around them the life of the city carried on, with trams, horses and carts, and motor vehicles passing within yards, but it was as though they were in their own little world. 'It's not good news, is it?' he said.

'No. It's Stella's granddad…he died two days ago. I thought you'd want to know, and this was the soonest I could get to Dublin.'

'Oh, Alice, I'm sorry. I'm really sorry for Stella, and…and I'm sorry for giving out when you've come all this way to tell me.'

Alice was touched by his pained expression, and she reached out and squeezed his hand. 'It's OK, Johnny.'

'Has the funeral happened yet?'

'Yes, he was buried in Canada. But they're having a memorial mass in Balbriggan tomorrow week.'

Johnny looked troubled again. 'God, Alice, I know Stella hates funerals – from when her brother died. I'd really like to be there, but I can't show up in Balbriggan.'

'She'll understand that.'

'I hope so. I'll…I'll write to her.'

'Do. That would mean a lot.'

'I'll write to her tonight.'

There was a pause, then Johnny looked at Alice. 'And how are you?'

'I'm fine.'

'Good. So, tell me all the latest with the band. I really miss our Friday nights.'

'The band's fine – though of course it's not the same without our star clarinet player.'

'What new tunes are you learning?'

'"The Old Folks at Home" and "Slattery's Mounted Foot".'

'Good songs.'

'They'd be no bother to you,' said Alice. 'But I have to really practise them.'

'And the Chess Club?'

'Still going strong. Robert Foley was back from Clongowes on midterm break and he went into a sulk when I beat him!'

'Nothing changes,' said Johnny with a grin.

'Yeah, he's still a pain!' Alice was pleased to see Johnny smiling and she was glad that they still had their old, easy friendship. But she couldn't ignore her anxieties, and after a moment she looked at her friend seriously. 'And what about you, Johnny? I know you can't tell me the details, but are you being careful?'

'I am.'

'Sure?'

'I promise I'm not taking stupid risks.'

'Good.'

'But it's…it's been a strange week.'

'What way, strange?'

Johnny hesitated, then answered quietly. 'I went back to St Mary's last Tuesday night.'

'Really?' Alice knew that Johnny was still marked by the cruelty he had suffered in the orphanage, and she was amazed that he had gone back.

'I went with Mr O'Shea,' said Johnny.

'I thought Mr O'Shea was in prison?'

'He escaped.' Johnny raised a hand. 'Don't ask me anything about him. I shouldn't really mention him at all.'

'OK.'

'But he came with me and he…he put manners on Brother Kenny.'

'Really?'

'Yes. And we got…we got what I'd always wanted.'

'You found out about your family?'

Johnny nodded. 'My father was foreign, he was a musician.'

'That explains a lot!'

'Yeah. And my mother's name was Norah Dunne. For some reason, they gave me her surname.'

Alice was fascinated, but she could see that Johnny looked troubled. 'Is she…is she still alive?'

'I think so. There was nothing to say she was dead. But I don't know if my father is dead or where he is. And I don't know why they put me in an orphanage.'

'Do you have an address for either of them?'

'Only for my mother. There's an address in Athlone.'

'That's…that's huge progress, Johnny. You can write to her, and then maybe meet up.'

'It mightn't be that simple. Supposing she isn't still at that address? Or supposing she doesn't want to meet me? And what am I to put in a letter? My head's been spinning the last few days.'

Alice thought a moment. 'Tell her that you've left St Mary's now. That you're in good health, and you're doing well.'

'And what about why they put me in the orphanage?'

'Don't blame her for anything, Johnny. I know you'd an awful time there, but you don't know how she was fixed. Maybe she thought she was doing the right thing. Maybe giving you up was the hardest thing she ever did in her life.'

'So, what do I say?'

'That you'd love to hear from her. And maybe after that you could meet. I know you want to know everything, but it might be best to go one step at a time.'

'Right…'

Alice could sense that Johnny's head was still reeling and she looked at him sympathetically. 'Would you like me to help you write the letter?'

'Would you?'

Alice was touched by the relief on his face and she smiled. 'Of course. What are friends for?'

Johnny smiled back. 'You're a brilliant friend, Alice. I'm sorry I'd to lie to you and Stella. But when this is over, we'll all get back together.'

'Of course we will. Meanwhile will we have a go at the letter?'

'That would be great.'

'All right,' said Alice, 'let's get started.'

CHAPTER TWELVE

Johnny lost himself in the music. He played 'Danny Boy' on the clarinet, injecting a hint of jazz into the rhythm, and improvising around the melody with his eyes shut. He was in the drawing room of Hanlon's boarding house where a cosy fire burned in the grate. The late October weather had turned cold, and this evening Mrs Hanlon had suggested swapping the chilly confines of his bedroom for practice sessions in the warmth of the drawing room.

He was grateful for her kindness at a time when his life was in some turmoil. It was five days since he had composed the letter with Alice, and he was anxiously awaiting a reply from Athlone. *If he ever got a reply from Athlone.* There was also the strain of not getting too friendly with the other telegraph boys, and misleading them about his reason for doing the job. Sometimes he played soccer with them at lunchtime in the yard behind the telegraph office. He had also joined the other boys in the shop, after they got paid their wages. He didn't want to spurn their friendship, particularly the outgoing Nedser, but the effort of never letting his cover story slip was stressful, and reluctantly he made a point of not getting too close to them. And then there was the need to be constantly on guard when trailing British intelligence agents.

Still, there was the satisfaction of playing an important part in the struggle for independence. And it was reassuring to know that his friendship with Alice and Stella was stronger than the many differences between them. He finished 'Danny Boy', opened his eyes and thought about what to play next. He had sheet music for 'The Rose of Tralee' in his satchel. But maybe something livelier would lift his mood. He opted for the music hall song 'In the Good Old Summer Time' and had begun to play its jaunty air when the door to the drawing room burst open.

'Mrs Hanlon,' said Johnny in surprise, 'what's—'

'The whole area's been cordoned off,' she said before he could finish his question. 'The Tans and the army are searching houses.'

'Right,' said Johnny, lowering the clarinet. 'But I'm registered as living here, so it should be OK.'

'The Boss isn't registered here. And he's on the premises.'

'Yeah?' Johnny had had no idea that Michael Collins was meeting Mrs Hanlon tonight. But one of the reasons Collins was so effective was that he kept himself a shadowy, elusive figure, who never stayed too long on one place.

'He's in my sitting room. We need to get him out of here fast. How would you feel about helping?'

'Absolutely.'

'He's going to leave by the back way and brazen it out at the first checkpoint he meets. Do you think you could brazen it out too? It would look more innocent if he's travelling with a young-ster.'

Johnny knew that the British didn't know what Collins looked like, and that the rebel leader believed in hiding in plain sight. But there was still risk involved in trying to get through the cordon. He felt his pulses starting to throb but he didn't hesitate. 'Count me in.'

'Sure?'

'Certain.'

'All right, there's no time to lose. Put on your good overcoat, and your best cap, and meet me at the back door.'

Johnny nodded, then he gathered his clarinet and music sheets, headed out of the room and ran up the stairs.

The October air was clammy and cold, and smoke billowed from countless chimney pots as the citizens of Dublin tried to keep warm. Stepping out into the laneway behind the boarding house, Johnny was well wrapped up in a woollen scarf and the good quality coat that Mrs Hanlon had bought him for the O'Shea escape bid. He had a snug-fitting boy's cap pulled down over his thick hair, and brown leather gloves on his hands. It was Mrs Hanlon's belief that a well-dressed person who looked middle-class would always seem less suspicious to the powers-that-be. Michael Collins obviously believed in the same theory, and he wore a soft hat and was smartly dressed in a tailored suit, over which he wore a fine Crombie overcoat.

'Leave all the talking to me, Johnny,' said Collins as they headed up the laneway towards Temple Street.

'OK.'

'And carry yourself confidently as though you haven't a care in the world.'

'Sure.'

'Good lad,' said Collins catching his eye and giving him a wink.

Johnny felt a boost to his confidence. Collins's self-belief was infectious. But it was one thing being brave – and even cocky – here in the laneway. How things went when they got to the cordon might be a different matter. Well, they'd know soon enough, he thought as they got to the corner of the laneway and turned onto the main road.

Sure enough, Mrs Hanlon's information had been correct, and a major search was taking place. Crossley tenders lined the street, and Tans and British troops were involved in a joint operation that involved searching houses, stopping vehicles and questioning pedestrians.

Johnny could see the cordon up ahead, between the Children's Hospital and St George's Church

'Don't slow down,' said Collins. 'Walk towards them and greet them warmly. We see this as a minor inconvenience, but we understand why it's necessary. We're on the side of law and order, and we back their efforts.'

'Right.'

Despite all the activity going on around them Collins chatted to Johnny about the coming feast of Halloween as they approached the checkpoint.

'Evening, Sergeant,' he said, stopping and nodding to the British soldier who stood blocking their way, his rifle at the ready.

'Evening, sir,' the man answered.

Sir, thought Johnny. Would the soldier have called him that if Collins had been dressed like a workman? An officer with a thin moustache and dressed in a captain's uniform drew near, but it was the sergeant who did the questioning.

'Name and address, please,' he asked in a strong Lancashire accent.

'Edward Taylor,' answered Collins, '27 Palmerston Road, Rathmines. And this is my nephew, Johnny.'

Following his earlier instructions, Johnny said nothing but smiled politely. He thought it was clever of Collins to pick an upmarket neighbourhood like Rathmines, and a name that could easily be Protestant.

'And your business in this area, Mr Taylor?'

Collins indicated the Children's Hospital. 'Brought Johnny to see a doctor.'

'At this hour?'

'Tied up with business during the day,' said Collins with a half apologetic smile. 'I arranged a private consultation for this evening.'

Johnny felt his heart pounding. If the soldier checked this story out they would be in deep trouble. But Collins sounded really plausible and unworried, and he hoped that the sergeant would buy the explanation.

'What's wrong with you, son?' the man asked, suddenly turning to Johnny.

'Tonsillitis,' answered Johnny deliberately making his voice hoarse.

The sergeant said nothing, and Johnny wondered if the man believed him. He was tempted to try to convince him, but he remembered his training with Mr O'Shea, who had taught him never to babble when being questioned. His pulses were racing, but Johnny said nothing further and tried to look unfazed.

After a moment the soldier nodded.

'Painful thing, tonsillitis. Had it meself as a nipper. I hope they get you sorted out.'

'Thanks,' said Johnny trying not to sound relieved.

The sergeant stood to one side to let them pass. Johnny moved forward, taking care not to appear too eager.

'Just one second,' said a voice, and Johnny anxiously turned around to see that it was the officer who had spoken.

'Palmerston Road, you say?'

If Collins was thrown by this late intervention he didn't show it.

'Yes, that's right.'

'Do you know the Conyngham family?' asked the officer in what Johnny recognised as an educated Dublin accent.

Johnny held his breath. If this was a trick question and Collins claimed to know a non-existent family the game would be up. But if the Conynghams were a well-known family and Collins *was* a resident of Palmerston Park, perhaps he should know of them.

Again Collins gave the apologetic smile. 'Sorry, can't say I know them.'

'Really? They're quite well established.'

'Well there you have it,' said Collins. 'I'm only a recent arrival.'

'I see. And where have you arrived from?'

'Cork. Most of our business has been in Cork, but we've expanded into Dublin.'

Smart again, thought Johnny. As an Irishman, the officer could probably tell that Collins was from Cork rather than Dublin.

'And what would that business be, Mr Taylor?

'Commercial Insurance. Plenty of claims, I'm afraid, since these damned rebels went on the rampage,' he added.

'Indeed,' agreed the officer.

Even though Collins had a prepared identity in his head, Johnny was impressed by how convincingly the rebel leader could improvise. The officer seemed to be convinced now, and Johnny allowed himself to relax a little.

'By the way,' said the officer. 'Why Temple Street?'

'As I explained to your sergeant, Johnny here has tonsillitis.'

'But you live on the south side. Harcourt Street Children's Hospital is nearer. Why cross the city to Temple Street?'

Johnny felt his pulses pounding again, and he prayed that Collins could come up with a convincing answer.

'It's a little further all right,' answered Collins. 'But one of the doctors is an old college pal who agreed to see us after hours.'

Johnny found himself holding his breath.

'Ah,' said the officer. 'The old school tie, eh?'

Collins smiled again. 'Something like that.'

'Very well, Mr Taylor. We'll detain you no further.' The Captain faced Johnny and nodded in farewell, 'Young man.'

'Evening, sir,' said Johnny.

Collins raised his hat to the officer. Then he placed a companionable arm around Johnny's shoulder and they walked off at an easy pace, away from the checkpoint and into the night.

CHAPTER THIRTEEN

Stella listened as the organ soared, the music seeming to swirl above the heads of the packed congregation in St Peter's church in Balbriggan. It was the Sunday morning of the memorial mass for her grandfather, and Mr Tardelli's playing of 'Nearer My God to Thee' was impassioned and moving. But Stella had cried all the tears she had in her, and now she simply squeezed back when Dad squeezed her hand in support.

Once the priest left the altar, Stella genuflected and stepped out into the aisle, followed by her father. Looking around, it seemed that every person she knew in Balbriggan was here. Alice and her mother were in the pew behind with many of the staff from the Mill Hotel, there were dozens of girls and teachers from her convent, the well-known local surgeon Dr Foley, and his son Robert, nodded to her, and her friends from the chess club and the town band were present in large numbers.

Stella wished that her mother could be here. Mom, however, had had to stay in Canada to wind up Granddad's affairs and wouldn't be back in Ireland for another couple of weeks. And even if Mom had been here, nothing could change the fact that Stella and her grandfather would never again share a joke, or have pancakes with maple syrup, or listen to his scratchy records.

There was a finality to his departure that Stella found frightening, and she was glad when she emerged from the church into bright October sunshine. She stood in the churchyard with her father, accepting condolences as the Sunday morning mass-goers milled about. She was touched by how many people took the trouble to offer their sympathies, even though some of them were republicans who opposed the British in the war of independence. She saw that some people were looking at her appraisingly as they offered their condolences and she suspected that they were surprised that she wasn't in tears. Could they not understand that she was really sad to lose her grandfather, but that by now she felt cried out?

She stood there for several minutes as adults and children alike mingled in the church yard, their demeanour lightening in many cases once they had offered their sympathy. Her father was chatting to Dr Foley, and she wondered how long more they would have to stay here when she heard a familiar voice.

'Hello, Stella.'

She turned around, and to her amazement saw Johnny Dunne. He had written her a lovely letter offering his condolence and apologising for the fact that he wouldn't be able to make it to Balbriggan for the mass. Yet now he was here.

'Johnny,' she said. 'I…I thought you…'

'I know,' he said. 'But I had to be here.'

Stella swallowed hard. She knew that Johnny had left Balbriggan in a hurry and that coming back was a risk for him. She knew too that he was more involved than ever with the rebels and was meant to be lying low while carrying out some secret mission.

But he had put all of that aside to be with her in her time of need.

'Oh, Johnny,' she said. 'I…I can't believe you came.'

'I couldn't not come,' he said simply.

'It's so good to see you. It…it means so much.' Stella looked at him, and suddenly, and to her surprise, her eyes welled up with tears.

Alice was shocked to see Johnny. She knew that the authorities weren't specifically looking for him – there had been too much chaos for the departure of a fourteen-year-old boots to attract much attention – but he was still taking a chance by showing up again. Alice tried to stand in her mother's line of sight, but Mam was too alert, and she suddenly stiffened.

She raised a hand to shield her eyes from the bright sunlight. 'Is that…is that Johnny Dunne?'

Alice looked over as though she had just noticed her friend. 'Yes. Yes, he must have travelled all this way to sympathise with Stella.' She hoped that by casting Johnny's visit in a positive light Mam might overlook her anger at Johnny for leaving his job at short notice.

'He's got a cheek showing up like this.'

'Mam…'

'Well, he has. Not a word from him since he left. And now he just turns up. If he expects to be welcomed back with open arms he's much mistaken.'

'Some hope!' Alice sounded sharper than she had intended and she raised her hand apologetically. 'Sorry, I didn't mean to snap. But I'm sure coming back had nothing to do with his job. It's hard for Stella being so far from Canada. I'm sure he just wanted to support her.'

Her mother shrugged. 'Maybe...'

'Please, Mam. I know you're annoyed at him. But don't say anything. Today isn't about you, or Johnny – it's about Stella's granddad.'

Her mother paused for a moment, then nodded. 'You're right.'

'Thanks, Mam. You don't mind if I go over and have a word with him?'

'I suppose not. I need to get back and check arrangements for the reception. Don't be too long, Alice, I could do with a hand.'

'All right.' Alice watched her mother go, then she crossed to where Johnny was chatting with Stella and Commander Radcliffe.

'Johnny,' she said, offering her hand as if they hadn't met since his departure. 'Good to see you again.'

'You too, Alice,' he said, shaking hands.

'Johnny was telling us about travelling up from Tipperary,' said Commander Radcliffe.

'Really?' said Alice. 'Good journey?'

'Yes, got the early train,' answered Johnny.

'Whereabouts are you working in Tipperary?' asked Commander Radcliffe.

'Thurles,' said Johnny.

'Thurles, eh? Do you like your new job?'

'Eh…yes, sir. Yes, it's fine.'

'And what exactly is your role?'

'Dad!' admonished Stella. 'You sound like you're cross-examining, Johnny.'

'Sorry, Johnny,' he said with a rueful smile. 'Occupational hazard for a commanding officer. Always asking questions.'

'It's grand,' said Johnny.

'Why don't I borrow Johnny, and let yourself and Stella mingle?' suggested Alice, feeling that she needed to get Johnny away from Stella's father. His enquiries were well-intentioned, but he was still a British officer, and Johnny would need to watch his every word to make sure he didn't give himself away.

'Thank you, Alice,' said Commander Radcliffe, 'a rock of sense, as ever. Nice to see you again, Johnny.'

'You too, Commander.'

'And good luck in the new job.'

All three friends exchanged a quick look, then Johnny nodded. 'Thank you. I'll see you before I leave, Stella,' he added as Alice led him away.

'OK.'

'Thanks for that,' said Johnny when they found a quiet spot near the far wall of the churchyard.

'I figured it might get tricky,' said Alice. 'So, you came in the end.'

'I had to. You and Stella have been brilliant friends. I couldn't stay away when she's lost her granddad.'

'It will mean a lot to her, Johnny.' Alice looked at him quizzically. 'Will you get in trouble with the people…the people you're working for?'

'They'd have a fit if they knew I was here. But I'm off on Sundays and they think I'm gone to a football match.'

'Right. And eh…any word from Athlone?'

Johnny shook his head. 'No. I'm…I'm not sure what to do next.'

'Well, it's only…what, about a week since you wrote?'

'It's a week exactly.'

'I'd wait a while.'

'And if she doesn't answer me?'

Alice could see the anxiety in Johnny's face and she kept her tone upbeat. 'If you hear nothing it doesn't mean she's not answering. She might have moved to another address.'

'I've no way of knowing that.'

'Well…you could always go to Athlone. It's on a train line from Dublin.'

'And do what? Check the house?'

'If it comes to that. But I bet it won't. I think she'll answer.'

'Maybe she'll answer that she doesn't want to see me. Maybe she's made a new life and won't want me showing up.'

'Maybe,' conceded Alice. 'But I doubt it. I just…I just feel it in my bones that it'll work out. And usually when I feel something in my bones, I'm right.'

'I really hope so, Alice.'

'Fingers crossed, then.'

'Yeah.'

'Would you like to come back to the Mill?' said Alice. 'Maybe we could play some music, and we're doing food and drink for all the mourners.' She knew that Mam wouldn't be happy about this, but she wanted Johnny to feel wanted.

'Thanks, Alice,' he said, 'but I'm already breaking all sorts of rules by showing my face here at all. Going to the hotel would be pushing my luck.'

'I miss the three of us making music, Johnny, and chatting and... and everything..'

'I do too. Badly, sometimes...'

'Are you sure you won't come back? You'd be really welcome.'

'Thanks. Alice, but I'd better just have a few words with Stella, and then get back to Dublin. Safer that way.'

'OK then. And talking of safety – be careful, Johnny. Please.'

'I will. Honestly.'

He said it reassuringly, but Alice feared that mightn't be possible, and that what he was doing was always going to be risky. 'I'll pray that you hear from Athlone,' she said. 'Let me know how you get on.'

'I will.' Suddenly he reached out and touched her arm. 'You're the best, Alice, you really are.'

Alice felt a lump in her throat. 'Johnny...'

'I mean it. I'll see you when I can.' He nodded in farewell, then crossed the churchyard towards Stella.

Alice stood unmoving, touched by Johnny's admission that he badly missed herself and Stella. It must be really hard for him, she thought, all alone in Dublin. Even though she sometimes argued with Mam, she knew she could always count on her support, just as Stella could count on her father. Johnny, though, had no such support, and Alice hoped that her prayers would come true and that Johnny's mother would answer his letter. Meanwhile she would continue to pray for his safety. It was all she could do for now and, watching him from across the churchyard, she hoped against hope that it would be enough.

CHAPTER FOURTEEN

Johnny cycled home excitedly. He had done a full day's work in the telegraph office, but in his eagerness to report to Mrs Hanlon he barely noticed the incline as he pedalled up Hill Street. The day had got off to a bad start when no letter had come from Athlone in the early morning post. Then he had heard the news that Terence MacSwiney, the jailed republican mayor of Cork, who was on hunger strike in Brixton Prison, was on the brink of death.

It had been shaping up to be a depressing Monday morning when Mr Williams had taken him aside in a quiet corner of the telegraph office.

'I've got an assignment for you, Johnny,' he had said.

'Fine.'

'We've a tip-off that two British agents are meeting in Café Cairo.'

'When is the meeting?' asked Johnny.

'They're there right now. You need to get over to Grafton Street and watch for when they leave.'

'Which one do I follow if they split up?'

'This one,' said Williams placing a photograph on the table before Johnny. It showed a heavy-set man in an officer's uniform. 'Don't worry about the first fella,' said William, 'we know where he lives. But if you could get this one's address that would be great. He's one of the few we haven't been able to pin down.'

'OK.'

'Be careful, Johnny. I can't emphasise enough that these agents are really dangerous.'

'I know. I'll watch my step.'

That had been this morning, and Johnny *had* watched his step, trailing his target very carefully when the two men had separated on leaving Café Cairo. Notwithstanding his caution he had had a bad moment when the man had suddenly done an about-face at the top of Grafton Street and walked back the way he had come. Johnny had been taken by surprise and his stomach had fluttered. He hadn't broken stride, however, and had walked towards the agent. He had tried to look as if he didn't have a care in the world, whistling 'Oh! Oh! Antonio' as he passed the man.

Had he been noticed? It was impossible to say, and an experienced agent would surely keep his face impassive if he did spot a tail. On balance though, Johnny felt that he would have just been another face in the crowd, and he had decided to continue following his target, although from further back. To his delight it had paid off when about twenty minutes later the man had turned into Hatch Street and let himself into a tall Georgian house. Johnny had noted the address, then continued with his normal day's work.

On returning to the telegraph office at lunchtime Johnny had discovered that Mr Williams had gone home sick with an upset stomach, which meant that he would instead be reporting his progress directly to Mrs Hanlon. Reaching the top of Hill Street now, he turned into Gardiner Place, then locked his bicycle to the railings outside the boarding house. He quickly ascended the steps, crossed to Mrs Hanlon's private parlour and knocked.

'Johnny,' she said opening the door and looking at him quizzically.

'I've something for you,' he said, unable to keep the satisfaction from his voice. 'Mr Williams had to go home sick, so I thought you'd want this. He handed her one of his telegram envelopes.

Mrs Hanlon raised an eyebrow. 'And this contains?'

'The address of the agent in the Café Cairo. The one you don't have.'

'Excellent. Where did you follow him to?'

'Hatch Street. He let himself in with a key, so I'd say he's lodging there.'

'Well done, Johnny, that's good work.'

'Thanks.'

'And you were, of course, discreet?'

Johnny thought of the moment when he had come face to face with the agent at the top of Grafton Street. But there was no point in worrying Mrs Hanlon with every little drama.

'Yes, I was very careful,' he said.

'Good lad. I've something for you too.'

'Oh?'

Mrs Hanlon went to the dresser then returned with a white envelope. 'This came for you.'

Johnny felt his mouth go dry. It had to be a reply from Athlone, nobody else knew his address here. He reached out, his hand shaky as he took the letter. 'Thank you.'

'I hope it's good news, Johnny. And I'm sure you want to open it in the privacy of your room.'

'Yes.'

'But before you do, there's something I need to say.'

Johnny's mind was whirling, but he forced himself to concentrate as Mrs Hanlon's steely blue eyes locked with his own.

'This is an exception, Johnny.'

'How do you mean?'

'Because of the circumstance – with the orphanage and so on – we've let you to use this address to try and contact your mother. But nobody else must know you're here. Nobody.'

'They don't.'

'It's vital you keep it that way.'

'I know.'

'Have I your word on that?'

'Yes.'

Johnny didn't like deceiving her, but he knew that she would never understand if he tried to explain about having met Stella and Alice again. And besides, the girls hadn't got this address. 'You have my word,' he said.

'Fine. And one last thing.'

'Yes?'

'If the news in your letter is good, if perhaps you make contact in time with family members – not a word of what you're doing here. Until your mission is over you've got to keep it absolutely secret.'

'I understand.'

'You're a great lad, Johnny. And after you've had a chance to read your letter, maybe you'll let me know how you got on?'

'I will.'

'Right, well, I'll leave you to it.'

'OK.' Johnny nodded, then left the room. He climbed the stairs rapidly, let himself into his room and sat down on the bed. His hand trembled as he opened the envelope and he hesitated, putting off the moment of truth. Then he unfurled the paper. The letter was two pages long and written in a good hand, and his mouth felt dry as he began to read.

Dear Johnny,

I'm so relieved that you're well and I'm sorry it's taken me several days to answer your letter. I've tried so many times to find the right words. But what words can explain to a son why his mother left him? All I can say is that leaving you was the saddest thing in my life. My heart was broken when I had to give you up, and when I got your letter I felt heart-broken again that we've lost fourteen years.

There's so much I want to tell you, but words on a page are not the right way, and I hope instead that we can meet in person. I'm also frightened to meet, because I think that part of you must surely be angry with me for giving you up, and if you are, no one could blame you. But if we're face-to-face I'll try to explain everything that happened, and why, and we can take it from there.

So could we perhaps meet next Sunday? I could get the eight o'clock train and be in Dublin by half nine. If that suits you we could meet in Kingsbridge station and maybe spend time in the Phoenix Park?

I can't believe that I've been given this second chance, Johnny, and I pray that we can get together. Please excuse me if I'm not saying all the right things. I'm not a great penwoman, but if I get a letter back saying you'll be in Kingsbridge all my prayers will have been answered.

I hope to see you then.

Your loving mother,

Norah Dunne

Johnny lowered the letter and sat unmoving on the bed. His emotions were in turmoil, having gone from fear of rejection to joy at his mother's desire to see him. He looked again at the phrase *your loving mother* and tears formed in his eyes. Then he turned back to the first page and, savouring every word, began to read the letter again.

CHAPTER FIFTEEN

'So what's going on with Johnny Dunne?'

'How do you mean?' answered Stella, knowing she had to be very cautious in responding. She was standing on the pavement with Alice and some of the other Chess Club members, warmly wrapped against the evening chill, and waiting for the club to open. The questioner was Esther Moore, the girl who had spotted Johnny cycling over O'Connell Bridge.

'I heard he was back in Balbriggan,' said Esther. 'That he was at your granddad's Mass last Sunday.'

'Yes, he travelled up, but couldn't stay long,' replied Stella.

'Why not?'

'He had to get back to Dublin.'

'So was I right about him working as a telegraph boy?'

'Eh…yes, that's what he's working at.'

'Even though he was supposed to be moving to Tipperary.'

'That was just temporary, Esther,' explained Alice, 'while he was waiting for the telegraph job to come through.'

'Right.'

Stella was relieved that her friend had come up with an explanation that Esther seemed to believe. Before she could relax, however, she saw Padraig Egan was looking at her appraisingly.

'So, Stella, what do you think of the death sentence on Kevin

Barry?' he asked.

Although the boy's tone was conversational, Stella knew that the question was hostile, and she hesitated. Kevin Barry was an eighteen-year-old rebel who had been captured after the killing of three British soldiers in Dublin the previous month. Stella had been upset by their deaths – partly because the death of any young man was sad, but also because it brought home to her that her father, as a British officer, could also be a target.

Kevin Barry had been sentenced to be hanged, and if the killing went ahead it would be the first execution of a rebel prisoner since the 1916 Rising. To make matters worse, Terence MacSwiney's hunger strike had ended with his death three days previously, and public feeling was running high.

She could see that the other club members were awaiting her answer to Padraig's question, and this time Alice couldn't rescue her. So far, most people that Stella encountered didn't hold it against her that her father was a British officer. But that could easily change, and now she chose her words carefully.

'I hope the death sentence isn't carried out,' she said.

'So you're for the rebels now, are you?' said Padraig.

'No. But I'm against the idea of hanging prisoners.'

'I hope so. Hanging a lad who's only eighteen – it's barbaric!'

Stella sensed that this was something that Padraig had heard others saying. She was actually more sympathetic to the rebels than she admitted to Padraig, but she wouldn't be publicly disloyal to her father. She hesitated, knowing that it might be wise not to argue further. Yet part of her felt that if she didn't say what she thought it would be cowardly.

She looked at Padraig, and his aggressive expression made her mind up. 'I'm sorry to see anyone of eighteen dying, Padraig. But either nobody of that age should die, or eighteen is old enough to be a soldier. It can't only be barbaric when someone Irish dies.'

'What are you saying?'

'Kevin Barry is eighteen, right?

'Yes.'

'And how old was Harold Washington, the soldier killed by Kevin Barry and his comrades?'

'I don't know.'

'He was nineteen. He was just a lad too.'

'That's different.'

'How is it different?'

'The English are occupying Ireland, and he's part of their army.'

'And the Irish are fighting them, and Kevin Barry's part of *that* army. Why is Kevin Barry's life more precious than Harold Washington's?'

'Because he's fighting for freedom.'

'They're *both* fighting for what they believe in. They're *both* in their teens. And I don't think you can say Barry is only a lad and it's barbaric to kill him – but then sing dumb about Washington's age. I mean, are you really saying it's wrong to kill a young man if he's Irish, but if he's English, that's OK, you can kill him?'

Stella could see the other club members looking to Padraig for a response, and she hoped that he might at least partially see her point.

He looked her in the eye then shook his head. 'You're just playing with words, Stella. Hanging Kevin Barry would be murder, and that's all there is to it.'

Before Stella could respond Mr Rooney arrived, ending the argument by unlocking the door and allowing the members to enter the chess club. Alice slipped her arm thought Stella's as they went in, and Stella was grateful for her friend's show of solidarity. She hoped that she had swayed some of the others with her arguments, but found it depressing that Padraig was blind to any viewpoint but his own. In reality, she thought there were probably equally unbending people on both sides, and perhaps that was the most disturbing thing of all. Dispirited by the notion, she made for the chess boards, hoping that for a few hours she could forget the troubles that raged all around them.

The trees in the Phoenix Park were a riot of colour, their leaves of gold, orange and red lit by the mellow sunshine of early November. It was ten o'clock on Sunday morning and the park wasn't busy yet, as Johnny sat at an outside table in the Victorian tea rooms. On the table before him were an iced bun and a cup of cocoa, but he had barely touched either item. 'I can't believe this is happening,' he said.

'I can't either,' said his mother, with a nervous smile.

His mother. The very phrase gave him goosebumps, and he looked at her now, fascinated by the resemblance between them. She too was slim, with blue eyes and brown hair, and the line of her nose and the tilt of her chin were startlingly similar to what Johnny saw when he looked in the mirror. She was younger than he had expected, probably only in her early thirties, and they had had no difficulty recognising each other when she stepped off the train for their arranged meeting at Kingsbridge station.

Johnny hadn't been sure how to greet her, and had offered his hand. She had smiled and shaken hands warmly, and in a voice that sounded shaky with emotion had told him how delighted she was to meet him. The short walk to the nearby Phoenix Park had been strange and slightly awkward, as though each of them was nervous of saying or doing the wrong thing.

She had told him that she lived in Athlone above the family's chemist shop, but that after the death of her mother earlier in the year the business had been sold. Her father had died three years previously, but she had a brother and four nieces and nephews.

Johnny found it bizarre to think that he had four cousins that he knew nothing of, as well as two deceased grandparents and an uncle.

Suddenly his mother put aside her cup of tea and looked at Johnny, her expression nervous. 'There's something I want to say, but...I don't know how to begin.'

'Well...take your time. There's no rush.'

'I know. But…we could go around in circles here, avoiding what really matters.' She paused, then reached out and touched Johnny's hand. 'I want to say I'm sorry. I'm so, so sorry, Johnny, that I gave you up.'

Johnny could see that tears had formed in her eyes and he kept his voice gentle as he asked that question that he had waited years to pose. 'Why did you give me up?'

'I'd no choice. I was only nineteen. A single woman with no means to support you. I would have done anything to keep you, but it just wasn't possible.'

'And what about my father? Where was he? And *who* was he?'

'He was…he was a wonderful man. I really loved him and we were going to elope and get married.'

'Elope?'

'He was a musician. My father didn't think that was a steady job, and didn't approve of him, so we planned to elope.'

'And why didn't you?'

'Josef was killed in a motor accident. A tram hit him, and he banged his head off the pavement. He died that same night from a brain haemorrhage. This was about seven months before you were born. Despite the fact that he had never met him, Johnny felt shocked to hear that his father was dead. 'God…that's terrible.'

'It was. His family was Hungarian, and he'd come to Dublin with an English orchestra. He liked Ireland and stayed on. I was a keen amateur musician, and that's how we met.'

'What do you play?'

'The piano. Josef played the violin. He was very good.'

'I play the clarinet,' said Johnny.

His mother gave a sad smile. 'So something of him lives on in you. I'm really glad.'

'I am too. And after he died, you never married anyone else?'

His mother shook her head. 'I was never going to meet someone that wonderful again. So I went back to Athlone and worked in the family business. My mother had poor health, and I ended up looking after her more and more.'

'That sounds hard.'

'I didn't mind. I had my music, and a job, and a roof over my head. And she was a good woman – I loved her. If it had been up to her, maybe something could have been worked out. But my father said keeping a baby would be a scandal, and I had to give you up. He said it would be best for the family, and for me, and even for you, to be put up for adoption.'

'But I wasn't adopted. I was just kept in an orphanage.'

'I'm really sorry, Johnny. They told me you'd get a good home, and I believed them. They said that I had to sever all ties, that I wouldn't be told where you went. They said it was better for everyone that way.' She paused, and when she spoke again there was a catch in her voice. 'But it wasn't better, was it?'

'No. Not for me.'

'Oh, Johnny,' she said. 'Can you…can ever forgive me?'

Johnny thought of his years in St Mary's. He thought of the beatings, and the cold, and the awful food. None of it need have happened if the Dunne family had taken him in, and he felt a flash of anger. He looked at his mother. A tear was rolling down her cheek, and he didn't know what to say as conflicting emotions swirled in his head.

'I understand if you're angry, Johnny. You've every right to be. *I'd* be angry if I was in your shoes. But I swear to you. If there was any way I could have kept you, I would have. I insisted they call you Dunne rather than Lazlo, so I'd always have some tiny link with you.'

Johnny looked her in the eye and he knew she was telling the truth. He felt his anger dissolving. *She had been young, and penniless, and probably scared out of her wits.*

'I'm not angry at you,' he said.

'No?'

'I wish I'd never known St Mary's. But it wasn't your fault.' He paused, touched by his mother's anguish. 'So...so everything's OK between us.'

She reached out and squeezed his hand. 'You've no idea what that means. Thank you so much.'

Johnny squeezed her hand in return, amazed at the idea that he was holding his mother's hand for the first time in fourteen years.

'So tell me all about your life now,' she said, brightening, and dabbing her eyes with a handkerchief.

'Gosh...where do I start?'

'Tell me about your job, and your friends, and playing the clarinet – I want to hear everything!'

Johnny considered for a moment, then told her about working in the Mill Hotel, and playing in Mr Tardelli's band, and becoming friends with Alice and Stella. He told her about the Tans burning Balbriggan, and how Stella had saved his life when she rescued him from the burning band hall. He would have loved to tell her the whole truth, but instead he kept secret his role in spying for the rebels, and explained that he had left Balbriggan to take up his current position, working as a telegraph boy.

'There's so much we have to catch up on,' his mother said.

'Well, we have all day.'

'I want to see you after today. I never want to lose contact again. If that's all right with you?'

'That's fine with me. But…there's just one thing…'

'What's that?'

'What should…what should I call you?'

His mother looked taken aback, as though she hadn't thought of this. 'Well…I always called my mother "Mam". Would that suit?'

Johnny nodded. 'Yes. Mam sounds…Mam sounds great.'

His mother looked at him, then rose and opened her arms. 'Come here and give me a hug.'

Johnny rose and crossed to her, and she took him in her arms. He caught the scent of her perfume as she embraced him.

'It's so good to see you, Johnny,' she said softly.

'It's so good to see you, Mam,' answered Johnny. Saying the word seemed to unleash something inside him, and the tears rolled down his face as he held his mother tightly.

CHAPTER SIXTEEN

Alice felt guilty as she listlessly chewed her steak in the dining room of the Mill Hotel. She knew that there were children in Balbriggan whose families could rarely afford meat – much less fillet steak – but she couldn't work up any enthusiasm for her food tonight. She was attending a dinner to welcome Stella's mother home from Canada, and seated with her at the table were her own mother, Stella, and Captain and Mrs Radcliffe.

The dining room of the Mill was busy with Saturday night customers, and her group was at the best table and receiving attentive service from the staff. It was a chilly November evening, but in here the atmosphere was cosy and warm. Alice looked around her, taking in the soft candlelight, crisp linen table cloths, gleaming cutlery and sparkling glasses, and she realised that the diners in the Mill were living in a bubble.

Outside the war was raging, and in the aftermath of Monday's execution of Kevin Barry there had been fighting in Longford, Galway, Waterford and Kerry, with civilians, police officers and British soldiers killed. How could so many of the customers here act as though nothing was happening, she wondered.

She toyed with her food, only half listening as Mrs Radcliffe described her sea voyage back from Canada. She was a smart, engaging woman with dark hair and sparkling eyes, and Alice liked her. But her fear was that Mrs Radcliffe would want Stella to move out of the Mill. It had been bad enough losing one friend when Johnny had left, but Alice hated the idea of also losing Stella, her closest friend and confidante, and she had worried about it for days.

'What's this I hear about Balbriggan being "adopted" by Philadelphia?' asked Mrs Radcliffe now.

'It's a way of showing support, Mom,' said Stella, 'because of all the buildings that were burned down.'

'I think it's more political than that,' said Commander Radcliffe. 'I daresay they want to help rehouse people, but I suspect it's also an anti-British move by Irish elements in America.'

'What does it matter, Dad, if it helps get Balbriggan rebuilt?' asked Stella.

'Politics *always* matters, dear, there's no getting away from it.'

'Well, maybe we can get away from it just for tonight,' suggested Mrs Radcliffe.

'I couldn't agree more,' said Alice's mother. 'Time enough for all the other problems. This is your homecoming night.'

'Fine. No politics tonight,' said Stella's father with a smile as he raised his hands in mock surrender.

The mood at the table was relaxed, and Alice sensed that this was the moment to pose the question that had been in her thoughts since the start of the meal.

'Can I ask a question, Mrs Radcliffe?' she said.

'Of course, Alice. What's on your mind?'

Alice hesitated, seeking to find the right words. 'I know it's your family, and I hope you won't think I'm intruding, but…'

'Yes?' said Mrs Radcliffe encouragingly.

'Will Stella be leaving now you're back? Or can she stay in the Mill for the rest of the school year? Please say she can stay, I'd really hate to lose her!'

Stella's mother looked a little surprised by the question and glanced at her husband. 'Well, we hadn't decided anything yet, Alice.'

'But I had asked Dad to let me stay in the Mill during term time,' said Stella.

'That was when I was away,' said Mrs Radcliffe.

'I know, Mom. And it's brilliant that you're back, and it'll be great spending weekends and holidays with you and Dad. But can I stay here during school term? I'd miss Alice as much as she'd miss me.'

Alice held her breath as she watched her friend's mother closely, hoping for a clue to her thinking. Once again Mrs Radcliffe glanced at her husband, who gave a little shrug that Alice hoped indicated acceptance. Stella's mother paused, and although it was only for a moment, to Alice it felt as she would never deliver her answer.

'All right, then. Maybe it would be best to see the school year out. After that we'll review things. Assuming that's acceptable to you, Mrs Goodman?'

'More than acceptable. Stella is welcome to stay as long as she likes.'

'OK, Stella?'

'Yes, that's great, Mom. Thanks.'

Mrs Radcliffe turned to Alice, a smile playing about her lips. 'Happy now, Alice?'

'Happy as Larry!' said Alice, playfully raising her glass of lemonade in a toast. 'Happy as Larry!'

Johnny walked along the edge of the cliff on Howth Head, the salt air bracing as he looked down at the glistening sea breaking on the rocks below him.

'I never tire of this view,' said his mother, indicating the sweep of Dublin Bay. 'No matter what season it is, any time I get to Dublin, I try to come out here.'

'Yes, it's great,' said Johnny. The heather-clad hillside before them looked beautiful in the autumn sunshine, while across the shimmering waters of bay could he could see the Wicklow mountains, their peaks etched against a clear blue sky.

Today was his second meeting with his mother, and with other day trippers they had gone on the train from Dublin to Sutton, and then taken the Hill of Howth tram to the summit of Howth Head. All week long Johnny had been looking forward to Sunday, and now he was savouring again the rapport they had established the previous week in the tea rooms.

There was so much for both of them to catch up on, and they had chatted non-stop on the train and tram. Johnny had discovered that his mother's favourite composer was Chopin, that her favourite food was apple tart, and that she was bad at sports, but good at swimming. He had revealed that he was good at soccer ,but not so good at swimming, that his favourite food was rice pudding, and that his favourite piece of music was 'Alexander's Ragtime Band' by Irving Berlin.

He had learnt that his father was gentle, but had a strong sense of humour. He had learnt also that Josef Lazlo was good at chess, and the fact that Johnny too was a skilful player made him feel bonded to the father that he had never met.

Standing on the cliff path, Johnny and his mother savoured the view across the bay for a moment more, then continued in the direction of the Baily Lighthouse.

'Tell me more about my uncle and my cousins,' said Johnny.

'You've four cousins, two boys and two girls. Michael is nine, Peg is seven, Sean is five and baby Cora is two.'

'Will I get to meet them?'

'Of course. My brother John isn't like my father was. When I wrote to John that we'd met again, he was really pleased.'

'And they're all in Athlone?'

'No, they're in Glasgow now. I telephoned John. Remember I told you we sold the chemist shop earlier this year?'

'Yes.'

'Well, the idea was that I'd stay on for several months, for a hand-over period. But John's best friend lives in Glasgow and he'd tipped him off about a bigger, better chemist's that was up for sale there. So John bought it. His wife Hannah – she'd be your Aunt Hannah now – and she's a lovely woman, you'll like her. Anyway, Hannah and the family are starting a new life with John in Scotland.'

'And are you going too?'

'The plan was that I'd join them this month. It was just pure luck I was still in Athlone when your letter came.'

'It would have been awful if you never got it.'

'Well, the new owner probably would have forwarded it. But I'm glad it never came to that.'

She looked at him, her expression appearing a little nervous. 'Now that we've had a second chance, Johnny, I don't ever want to lose you again. I'd…I'd like us to be together. How would you feel about that?'

'I'd like it. I don't want to lose you again either.'

His mother smiled. 'Good. Obviously we'll take it a step at a time, but we should talk about the future.'

'Yeah.'

Part of Johnny was exhilarated that his mother was so keen to have him in her life. And it was great to no longer be rootless, and to know who his father was, and to have cousins and an uncle and aunt. But another part of him was anxious. He had a mission to accomplish for Michael Collins, and he couldn't pull out of it now.

He looked across Dublin Bay, its calm beauty belying the chaos and the killing that was going on in the city. Maybe he could stall his mother a little, finish his mission without her knowing, and then start whatever future they were to have. But that would mean beginning their relationship with a lie, and he didn't want that.

He walked along the trail, his thoughts a jumble. He *could* swear his mother to secrecy, and tell her about his mission. But he had already seriously breached the rules by telling Stella and Alice that he was working undercover. Mrs Hanlon knew he had made contact with his mother, and she had reminded Johnny again about the need for the utmost secrecy until the mission was over.

'You've gone very quiet, Johnny.'

'Sorry, I just…I was just thinking.'

'It's a confusing time,' said his mother gently. 'Take as long as you need to think about it all.'

Johnny was touched by her concern and he felt a strong urge to come clean. Yet if he did he would be breaking the trust of Collins and Mrs Hanlon. He understood the need for secrecy – they were involved in a life and death struggle where one slip could mean capture, and where even a prisoner as young as Kevin Barry could be executed. But was his mother really a security risk? From her comments about the Black and Tans it had been clear that her sympathies were with the rebels. He walked on in silence, his head swimming from his conflicting urges.

Suddenly he came to a halt and turned to face his mother. He paused, trying to marshal his thoughts.

'What's wrong?' she asked

'If I…if I tell you something, will you promise to tell nobody?'

'Of course.'

'It's really, really important. You have to swear you'll tell no one.'

'All right, Johnny. If it matters that much, then I swear.'

'I shouldn't be saying this,' said Johnny, 'but I don't want any lies between us. When I…when I worked in the Mill Hotel in Balbriggan I was spying for the rebels.'

'What?!'

'Lots of RIC and British officers drank in the Mill. I listened in on what they said and passed it to the IRA.'

'Oh my God, Johnny! That's a dangerous game.'

'No more dangerous that what other people are doing to free Ireland.'

'They're not fourteen years old.'

'I know. But this was something I wanted to do. The thing is…I'm still working for them.' He saw the confusion on his mother's face.

'I thought you were working for the telegraph office.'

'I am, but that's a cover. I'm carrying out a mission. I can't tell you anything about it. They'd go mad if they knew I'd told you this much. So please, don't ask me what I'm doing.'

'But it's something dangerous, isn't it?'

'I'm being extremely careful.'

She looked him in the eye. 'I can't tell you what to do, Johnny – I lost that right a long time ago. But your life is precious. It would be unbearable if anything happened to you. Especially now we've been given this second chance.'

'I know.'

'I want us…I want us to have a future together.'

'So do I. So I won't take any more risks than I have to. But I've got to see this out – it's only for a few more weeks. All right?'

'If…if that's what you really have to do.'

'It is. Absolutely.'

'All right then,' she said reluctantly. 'And Johnny?'

'Yes?'

'Thank you for sharing this with me.'

'I want us to be straight with each other.'

'We will be. Always. Meanwhile, there's a lot of stuff we need to think through.'

'Will we do it as we walk?'

'Yes, let's do that.'

'After you,' said Johnny. He breathed out, relieved that he had taken the plunge, then he happily followed his mother along the sunlit path.

CHAPTER SEVENTEEN

'I wish we didn't have to go to this service, Mom,' said Stella.

'We have to, for Dad's sake.'

'I know. I just...'

'Just what?' said her mother gently.

They were in Stella's room in the Mill Hotel, the atmosphere warm and cosy compared to the chilly November air outside. Her mother was putting the finishing touches to plaiting Stella's hair, and they were preparing to attend an Armistice Day service in Dublin, once they had been picked up by Commander Radcliffe.

'I feel a bit torn, Mom.'

'How, torn?'

'With all the awful stuff with the Black and Tans. It's hard not to sympathise a bit with the rebels. I mean, would it really be that bad if Ireland got independence?'

Her mother considered for a moment. 'The politics are complicated, Stella. But the way they're going about independence, killing and shooting people, that's not the civilised way to bring change.'

Stella wondered if there *was* a civilised way to win independence, but she said nothing.

'Besides,' said her mother, 'Armistice Day is about commemorating those who fell in the Great War. It's a separate thing.'

'Not to some people here. They think it's all the British Empire, ruling the roost and flying the flag.'

'Don't say that in front of your father, Stella. Armistice Day is important to him; he lost friends in the war.'

'I wouldn't dream of it, Mom. I'm just saying what the mood is with some people.'

'What people?'

'Folks in Balbriggan. In the chess club, and the band, and girls talking in school. They're not saying stuff to me because Dad is an officer, it's just what I hear.'

Her mother finished the hair plaiting and shifted position to look Stella in the eye. 'In spite of all that, you were very keen to stay in Balbriggan.'

'I know. And thanks again for letting me stay.'

'So, what's really going on, Stella?'

'How do you mean?'

'Have you some other reason for wanting to stay in Balbriggan?'

Stella swallowed hard. She thought about the secret shared by herself, Johnny and Alice, but tried to give nothing away by her expression. It was lovely to have her mother back from Canada, but Mom was more aware than Dad had been, and Stella realised she would have to be careful.

'I want to stay for all the reasons I gave you, Mom,' she said.

'Is there…is there a boy involved?'

'No.'

'I'd understand if there was, Stella. I was thirteen once too.'

'I don't have a boyfriend, Mom.'

'All right. Though I believe Johnny Dunne came back specially for Granddad's mass.'

'It's not like that with Johnny. He's just a friend. A really good friend, but that's all.'

'OK.'

'And he's not around here any more, he has a job back in Dublin,' added Stella, deciding to play down the link to Johnny as much as possible.

'Right.'

'I like living in Balbriggan, it feels…it feels like home now, Mom, in a way Toronto never did.'

'Really?'

'I love Mr Tardelli's band, and the chess club, and my classmates, and living in the same place as Alice. It's good here, Mom, despite what happened the town.'

'If you say so.'

Stella sensed that her mother wasn't fully convinced, but before she could respond there was a knock on the door.

'All present and correct?' said Commander Radcliffe good humouredly as he stepped into the room.

Stella looked at her father, resplendent in his RAF dress uniform, and she felt a flood of affection for him. She wished, yet again, that Johnny and Dad didn't have to be on opposite sides, and on impulse she crossed to him and kissed him on the cheek. Then she linked his arm and made for the door, determined to show her support, as they went to mark Armistice Day.

* * *

'So, boys and girls, a question for you,' said Mr Tardelli playfully.
'What's the result if you drop a piano down a mine shaft?'

Alice wracked her brains, knowing the joke would have some
sort of musical basis. It was break time in band rehearsal at the
church hall, and although everyone groaned at Mr Tardelli's riddles and jokes, Alice knew that most of the band members actually
enjoyed them.

She looked at Stella, who shrugged to indicate that she hadn't
a clue regarding the answer. Alice could think of nothing either,
and she turned to the musical director. 'All right, Mr T. What's the
result when you drop a piano down a mine shaft?'

Mr Tardelli kept a straight face, but Alice could see that his eyes
were twinkling.

'A flat minor!' he answered.

There was the usual mixture of laughter and groans, but Alice
thought the joke was actually quite clever.

'I've another music joke,' said Padraig Egan.

'Go on then,' said Alice. She didn't like Padraig when he spouted
the political the views that he clearly heard at home, but most of
the time he was good fun, and he knew how to tell a joke.

'What's a cat's favourite song?' he asked.

'What?'

'Three Blind Mice!'

Alice laughed with the others, then Padraig changed the mood with a question to Stella.

'So, what did you think, when Sinn Féin protested during Armistice Day?' he asked.

Mr Tardelli encouraged wide-ranging discussion during rehearsal breaks, and he didn't chide Padraig for altering the relaxed atmosphere, but Alice thought Padraig was being mean-spirited. She didn't immediately spring to Stella's defence, however, feeling that it was important to let her friend be seen standing up for herself.

Stella thought for a moment then answered in an even tone. 'Armistice Day is to honour the war dead, so I thought it was rude to start chanting during the proceedings.'

'But it's not just honouring the dead, is it?' answered Padraig. 'They're glorifying the war.'

'You wouldn't like it if someone came to a friend's funeral and chanted slogans. It's just bad manners, Padraig, to chant when people are mourning their dead.'

'If they were worried about the dead they shouldn't have let thirty-thousand Irishmen be killed fighting England's war.'

'No one said the losses weren't terrible,' said Stella. 'But there's a time and a place to make your protest.'

'There might be if the government were honest,' answered Padraig. 'If they said the slaughter was a tragedy. But they don't say that. They fly their flags, and parade, and *glorify* the war on Armistice Day. So it's only right that people *protest* on Armistice Day.'

Alice felt that Padraig had a point, even if he was parroting an argument that he had heard from others.

'I actually agree with you about the glorifying part,' said Stella. 'They should stop that and concentrate on mourning. But chanting slogans? I still say it's wrong to protest like that.'

'It's freedom of speech,' said Padraig.

'You can have freedom of speech without being nasty.'

Alice didn't want to see the discussion turning into a row and so she turned to Mr Tardelli, who often joined in their discussions. 'What do you think, Mr T?' she asked.

The musical director stroked his moustache as he seemed to gather his thoughts. 'I'm torn,' he said. 'I believe it's important to respect the dead. But I think Padraig is right. I think the government use Armistice Day to glorify the war.'

'Even if they do, Mr Tardelli,' said Stella. 'Is it not plain bad manners to chant when people are mourning the dead?'

'Yes, Stella, it feels that way to me. But then we have to ask ourselves a hard question.'

'What's that?' asked Alice.

'Do we just allow freedom of speech when people say what we like? Or do we allow it when they say things we hate? And if they can't say things we hate, it's not really freedom of speech, is it?'

'Maybe,' said Alice.

'But where do you draw the line?' asked Stella.

'I'd draw it at chanting,' said Mr Tardelli. 'But others don't, and maybe we should keep an open mind. But now, I think we've talked enough. Back to the music!'

Alice looked at Stella, and winked to show her solidarity. Then she picked up her violin, her thoughts a muddle as she grappled with all that had been said.

Johnny watched his target carefully, allowing the man to get a hundred yards ahead before mounting his bicycle and following him. The agent had come out of Rabiatti's Saloon on Marlborough Street, one of the meeting places of the British intelligence officers operating in Dublin. Up until now Johnny had found his undercover work nerve-wracking yet exciting, but today he felt less excited and more on edge.

Johnny had been warned that the man he was following, Captain Bennett, was a key member of the enemy intelligence team sent to Dublin to combat Michael Collins. But it wasn't just the thought of dealing with an experienced foe that had Johnny feeling uneasy. The previous night the authorities had launched a major operation in the north inner city. People had been questioned, houses searched, and from his room several streets away in Gardiner Place, Johnny had heard shots fired. The search hadn't extended to Hanlon's boarding house, but the thoroughness and size of the operation had taken Johnny aback. He realised that at any time the enemy might cast their net again, and that next time he mightn't escape their attention. It was wearying, too, having to be constantly on guard, and it went against his nature not to be friendlier with the other telegraph boys.

Mr O'Shea had told him that his mission would be ending soon, and although he hadn't admitted it, Johnny had felt relieved. More importantly, though, his world had changed since meeting his mother, and the previous Sunday they had taken the steam tram to Lucan, then travelled by jaunting cart along the Liffey Valley to the Strawberry Beds. It had been a crisp autumn day, and as with his other two meetings with his mother, he had come home that evening exhilarated, and feeling there was more to live for than the struggle for independence

He still wanted to play his part in changing Ireland. Only this morning he had seen in the newspaper headlines that the Bolshevik revolutionaries had won the civil war in Russia, so change was possible. Not that he was so naive as to think that change was always good – there was no telling how the Bolsheviks would work out. He had read too that his comedy hero, Charlie Chaplin, had been divorced, and that was hardly a positive change. But he still wanted to bring about a better Ireland, and today his orders were to follow Captain Bennett and to take note of anyone with whom he made contact.

Johnny cycled down a blustery Marlborough Street, closing the gap on Bennett, then dismounted when he was about twenty yards behind his target. He went through the motions of opening his telegram satchel, and he allowed the English officer to widen the gap again. Johnny distractedly flicked through the telegrams, as though seeking one in particular. In truth he *was* a bit distracted today, his mind still grappling with what his mother had said at their last meeting.

She had nervously proposed that when Johnny's mission was finished he could live with her in Glasgow. Johnny had been moved by her desire for them to be together and touched too by the fact that it meant so much to her that she was nervous about his response. She had told him to take his time and think about it, and Johnny had thanked her and said that he would. Part of him felt that he should stay in Ireland and see to the finish the fight for independence. Another part of his brain told him that he had already taken big risks, and that maybe his current mission should be his last one. It was, after all, the course of action that Mr O'Shea had suggested. He felt too that he was blessed to get an unexpected chance at having a family life. He loved the idea of being part of an extended family with his mother, his uncle and aunt, and his cousins, and he thought that maybe he should seize the opportunity.

Before he could deliberate any further Johnny saw Captain Bennett turning the corner into Abbey Street. He quickly put the telegrams back into his satchel, then lifted his bicycle onto the pavement and wheeled it towards the corner. Just as Johnny reached the junction with Abbey Street, Bennett came back around the corner. The manoeuvre caught Johnny unawares and for a moment Bennett locked eyes with him. Johnny got a fright and he hoped his surprise didn't show on his face. It wasn't the first time that those he had been trailing had taken evasive action. Most times, however, he was far enough behind not to be noticed, and when he had encountered the agent who doubled back at the top of Grafton Street, Johnny had whistled as though unconcerned and strode past him.

This felt different though. It was possible that Bennett saw nothing suspicious in a telegraph boy with whom he exchanged a glance. But the British officer was a trained agent. And not alone was he a professional, he was an agent working in a highly challenging environment, where every chambermaid, every barman, every hotel receptionist – in fact just about every civilian – was a potential enemy agent against whom he had to be on guard. *And he had seen Johnny clearly*.

Johnny kept going now, resisting the urge to look behind him to see what Bennett was doing. Instead Johnny turned the corner into Abbey street and walked along at a moderate pace as he considered his next move. Should he circle around and continue to follow Bennet from a distance? Or would it be smarter to cut his losses and call off today's mission?

It went against the grain to call a halt. But if Bennett spotted him for a second time, alarm bells would surely ring. Johnny remembered his promise to Alice that he wouldn't take needless risks. And now that he had found his mother again there was even more at stake. He stopped wheeling the bicycle and opened his satchel again, going through the telegrams as he tried to reach a decision.

Supposing this was the day when Bennett met an informer that the rebels hadn't been aware of? Yet it could also be the day when Johnny gave the game away by pushing his luck – and if that happened he would be endangering Mr O'Shea and Mrs Hanlon. He hoped he wasn't fooling himself with these arguments, and that he wasn't simply losing his nerve now that he had more to live for.

He stood unmoving on the pavement for a moment, uncertain what to do. Then he decided to follow his gut instinct. He recalled the observant look in Bennett's eyes when they had exchanged glances, and it made his mind up. Calling off the mission, he wheeled his bicycle to the roadway, mounted the saddle and cycled briskly away.

CHAPTER EIGHTEEN

Alice watched as the wrecking ball smashed into the side of the building. It sent shattered brickwork and plaster in all directions, but Alice and her mother observed from a safe distance. Part of her couldn't help but enjoy the drama of seeing the building being demolished, but she mostly felt sad that Balbriggan had so many vacant sites where the burnt-out houses and shops stood. Some rebuilding had already begun, and eventually families whose homes were ruined would be re-housed, but Alice wondered if the hundreds of workers who had lost their jobs at the destroyed Deeds Templar factory would ever find work again.

The burning of the town had received extensive coverage in the newspapers, and questions had even been asked in parliament in Westminster. Mam had said that a Commission of Enquiry had been set up to investigate what was being called the Sack of Balbriggan. But even Mam, who was normally pro-government, said she wouldn't hold her breath waiting for its findings.

'I think we've seen enough, Alice', she said now, as the wrecking ball swung again, knocking down a wall and raising a cloud of dust.

'Yes,' agreed Alice, slipping her arm through her mother's as they turned away and began walking home. It was a misty November afternoon, and they stepped over sodden leaves as they made their way towards the Mill. The light was starting to fade, and the slightly gloomy atmosphere created a sense of intimacy. It seemed to Alice the right moment to ask a question that had been on her mind, and she turned to her mother and spoke softly. 'Just between ourselves, Mam. Who do you honestly think is going to win the war?'

Her mother looked surprised by the question. 'Well, you know I've always favoured law and order.'

'But the Tans and Auxies haven't brought law and order, have they?'

'No,' admitted her mother, 'they haven't. On the other hand, the rebels have created chaos. That's hardly to be admired either.'

'So who do you think will win?'

'Why are you asking this now, Alice?'

'Because it will affect us in the Mill. More and more people are for the rebels, Mam. If they win, we'll need to adjust.'

'But if they're *not* the winners we mustn't burn our bridges. The government may decide the rebels must be beaten at any cost.'

'So you think the rebels will lose?'

'I honestly don't know, Alice. It could go either way. Meanwhile we have to do a tricky balancing act.'

'Lots of girls in school are for the rebels and a new Ireland.'

'But what sort of an Ireland would that be? An Ireland whose leaders would be gunmen?'

Alice thought of Johnny, who was risking his life to bring about a better country. 'Maybe it would be a good Ireland, Mam. Run by people with ideals.'

'That remains to be seen. Meanwhile we take it a day at a time, and keep our heads down. All right?'

'Right,' said Alice. But she knew that Johnny wasn't keeping his head down, and she prayed that he was safe as she trudged home through the darkening November streets.

'I'm sorry, Mr O'Shea, but I think that's plain silly,' said Johnny.

He was in Mrs Hanlon's private parlour, to which she had invited him to play the clarinet for herself and Mr O'Shea. The room was warm and comfortably furnished, and the atmosphere had been relaxed. Now, however, the mood had been broken by O'Shea chiding Johnny for playing 'Hold Your Hand Out, Naughty Boy', a music hall song that he claimed was very English.

'There's nothing silly in preferring Irish music to the music of the oppressor,' said O'Shea.

'I play lots of Irish music,' said Johnny. 'But "Hold Your Hand Out" is a catchy tune and good fun. What of it, if it's English?'

'They're the enemy.'

'Not their music. And not even everyone English, Mr O. I mean, we're fighting their army, not the whole English race.'

'We're fighting everything they stand for, Johnny. We have our own culture, they have theirs. It's better not to mix the two.'

Johnny had a lot of respect for Mr O'Shea and had never seriously argued with him before. He looked to Mrs Hanlon, who, although a committed republican, tended to be more liberal. She didn't say anything, but gave Johnny a tiny wink, which he took to be encouragement to argue his corner with O'Shea.

'I'm sorry, Mr O'Shea, but I don't agree. Do you remember Mr Tardelli, who ran the band in Balbriggan?'

'Yes,' answered O'Shea. 'What's that got to do with anything?'

'Mr Tardelli is Italian. In the Great War Italy fought against Germany. For three years they were the enemy. But Mr Tardelli didn't stop playing music by Beethoven, because Beethoven was German. Are you really saying he should have? Or that English mothers shouldn't have sung Brahms' Lullaby to their babies, because Brahms was German?'

O'Shea didn't answer at once, and Johnny detected a faint smile from Mrs Hanlon.

'I think maybe you should be a barrister, Johnny, when all this is over,' she said. 'Talking of which,' she added, looking meaningfully at O'Shea.

He nodded, then turned to Johnny. 'Let's agree to differ about the music. There's something else we need to talk about.'

'OK,' said Johnny. He was a little disappointed that O'Shea was so rigid that he couldn't be swayed, but relieved too that he hadn't taken exception to being bested in an argument by a fourteen-year-old.

'We want you to check the whereabouts of someone on Saturday night, Johnny,' said O'Shea. 'But after that your mission will be over.'

'Really?'

'You've done a great job,' said Mrs Hanlon. 'You can really be proud of yourself.'

'Thank you,' said Johnny. 'So, after Friday…what happens?'

O'Shea hesitated, choosing his words carefully. 'What we've been working towards for the past couple of months is about to come to a head. I can't give you any more details. The less you know, the safer it is for you.'

'For the rest of the weekend, Johnny, you'll need to lie low,' said Mrs Hanlon. 'Don't ask me why, but it's important you do.'

'All right. And after that?'

'A lot depends on how things go,' said O'Shea. 'We might need to get you out of Dublin for a while.'

'You've done more that your share, Johnny,' said Mrs Hanlon. 'Maybe it's time to get to know your mother better and live the normal life of a boy your age.'

Johnny's mind was racing, and he wasn't sure how to respond.

'We don't have to decide the details right now,' said O'Shea. 'But your mission is ending, and I want to thank you, really sincerely, for all you've done.' He rose and crossed to Johnny, offering his hand. 'God Save Ireland.'

Johnny stood up, and they solemnly shook hands. 'God Save Ireland,' he said.

PART THREE

TURMOIL

CHAPTER NINETEEN

Johnny cycled through the city streets, on full alert for this, his final mission. Now that the end had almost come any kind of mistake would be disastrous, and he was determined that nothing should go wrong this evening. Saturday nights in town were always lively, but tonight the streets were busier than usual, with Tipperary supporters gathering outside pubs and cafes ahead of tomorrow's football match against Dublin in Croke Park.

For weeks Johnny had avoided thinking about what would happen to the men whose movements he had tracked so carefully. Now, though, the moment of truth had arrived. Although Mr O'Shea hadn't spelled it out, Johnny was sure that this weekend the IRA was going to strike against the British agents. How would he feel if some of the officers he had spied on were killed? The more time he had spent trailing them, the more he had found himself thinking of them as people rather than targets. He knew Mr O'Shea would say that Collins' intelligence network had to be protected at all costs. The British agents were planning to eliminate their Irish opponents, and in war it was kill or be killed. But Johnny still felt uneasy now that violence was about to be unleashed.

He went past the Shelbourne Hotel, its windows aglow with soft yellow light as he cycled through the dark November evening.

He turned right along St Stephen's Green, thinking yet again on what Mrs Hanlon had said about having a normal life with his mother once his mission finished. He was still slightly uncomfortable with ending his part in the fight for independence before the campaign was over. But if Mrs Hanlon and Mr O'Shea both felt that he had more than played his part, then maybe he had.

Reaching Leeson Street, he dismissed the thought, knowing he would need to have his wits about him fully as he neared his destination. Cycling on, he saw ahead the sign for The Eastwood Hotel and he slowed down, gathering himself. His task was to establish if Lt. Colonel Jennings was staying overnight in the hotel, but he had to do it without arousing suspicion. He dismounted from the bicycle and leaned it against a lamppost. He walked up the steps and entered the hotel, adopting the casual demeanour of a telegraph boy who has done dozens of similar deliveries. He knew that his uniform gave him credibility and he spoke confidently to the receptionist on reaching the desk.

'Good evening,' he said. 'Lt. Colonel Jennings staying here tonight?'

If he wasn't, then Johnny would report that information back to Mrs Hanlon. If he was, Johnny would go through his satchel, only to apparently discover that the telegram for Jennings was missing. He would promise to collect it from the telegraph office and return later. Instead he would report to Mrs Hanlon, confirming the presence of the British officer.

'Yes, he's staying overnight with a couple of friends,' answered the receptionist, a middle-aged woman with a friendly manner. 'In fact, they've just gone into the dining room. Do you want to give him the telegram?' Johnny hadn't been expecting this, and he hesitated briefly. 'Or you can leave it with me,' suggested the receptionist.

'I'll drop it in to him myself,' said Johnny.

'Round the corner, past the stairs. Glass doors straight in front of you for the dining room,'

'Thanks,' said Johnny, then he moved away from the desk and began opening his satchel, as though seeking the telegram for Lt. Colonel Jennings. He rounded the corner, then slowed down, pausing when he reached the dining-room door. He would need to wait a moment, so that it appeared to the receptionist that the he had delivered the telegram.

He pretended to sort through his satchel, then glanced though the glass doors. The dining area had tables set with crisp white linen and gleaming cutlery, and the room was busy, with uniformed staff tending to well-dressed guests as they had dinner. Johnny immediately spotted Jennings, recognising him from when he had tailed him previously. He was seated at a table with two other men. None of them was in uniform, but their appearances suggested to Johnny that all three were officers.

He was about to turn away when the member of the trio with his back to Johnny leaned forward to pour water into his glass. Something about him seemed familiar, and Johnny stopped, then moved a little further to the right to get a better view. Now he saw the man's face, and Johnny quickly stepped out of his line of vision, shocked to discover that Stella's father, Commander Radcliffe, was one of Lt. Colonel Jennings's guests.

Johnny stood unmoving, his mind reeling. Could Stella's father be a spy too? Surely not, he had a full-time job as a Wing Commander in the RAF. But why was he meeting a spy like Jennings? And what would happen Commander Radcliffe if the IRA came for Jennings?

Johnny turned away and made for the hotel exit, trying to keep his expression normal as he returned the greeting of the receptionist. He descended the steps to the roadway. The air felt cool after the warm interior of the hotel, but Johnny barely noticed. The more he thought about it, the less likely it seemed that Stella's father was a spy. A more convincing explanation was that he knew Jennings from the past. Maybe they had grown up in the same part of England, or perhaps they had served together during the Great War. But none of those thoughts lessened the sick feeling that Johnny had in his stomach. *If Jennings was going to be killed at the Eastwood Hotel, Commander Radcliffe could easily be killed with him.*

Johnny mounted his bicycle, automatically going through the motions of pedalling and steering while his mind raced. He had overheard Mr O'Shea and Mrs Hanlon talking about everything being co-ordinated for nine a.m. They had also told him he would have to lie low for the rest of the weekend. That suggested that action against the British agents was scheduled for nine o'clock tomorrow morning.

Staying overnight with a couple of friends was what the receptionist had said. And Johnny knew from talking to Stella that sometimes her father did stay overnight with friends, rather than travelling back to either Baldonnel or Balbriggan.

Somehow he had to warn Commander Radcliffe. Yet if he did, he would be betraying Michael Collins, and Mr O'Shea and Mrs Hanlon. And a mission that had taken months of preparation would be ruined. On the other hand, if her father were killed, could he ever again look Stella in the eye? She had risked her life for him, and he would have burned to death in Balbriggan but for her bravery.

He had to do something, he knew, yet every choice seemed to involve betraying someone. He cycled towards home, the streets and the people a blur, as he grappled with the biggest decision of his life.

CHAPTER TWENTY

'Penny for your thoughts,' said Alice playfully.

Stella looked at her friend and smiled ruefully, aware that her mind had been drifting. They were having an early Sunday morning breakfast before setting off for a hockey match. Stella's mother had stayed in an adjacent room last night – Dad was meeting some old comrades in Dublin – and Mom had opted for a lie-on this morning. The dining room of the Mill was quiet, but Stella pushed aside the remnants of her fry and leaned closer. 'I was thinking…if only things were clear cut,' she said. 'Instead… everything's confusing.'

'Are you talking about Johnny?' asked Alice, lowering her voice

'Not just Johnny – the whole thing. No matter what side I take it's like I'm disloyal to somebody.'

'It's tricky all right,' agreed Alice. 'So right now, where do you stand?'

'I don't know. I'm Canadian, Mom is French-Canadian, Dad is English, my friends are Irish. Who am I supposed to support?'

Alice shrugged sympathetically. 'If it's any consolation, I'm torn too. When I think about what the Tans and the Auxies did to Balbriggan, I'm for the rebels. But then someone like your dad is dead sound. And lots of the British officers who use the Mill are really nice. It's hard to see them as the enemy.'

'It's even harder for me, Alice. When I listen to Dad, I'm swayed by his arguments. But when I think about what Johnny's said, I see his point too.'

'It's not just who's right or wrong though, is it?' said Alice. 'You also have to weigh up who's going to win.'

'And right now, who would you say that is?' asked Stella, not sure what she wanted to hear as an answer.

Alice thought a moment before answering. 'Probably the government, if they're really ruthless. But maybe the rebels, if the government feel they can't go to war against the whole Irish nation, or a big majority of them.'

'So where does that leave me?'

'Maybe the best you can do is go with your instinct, but accept that there are good people on both sides.'

Stella thought that sounded sensible and she nodded in agreement. But where her instincts might take her was anybody's guess, and she finished her tea absent-mindedly, wondering where it would all end.

Johnny wiped a bead of sweat from his forehead as he cycled towards The Eastwood Hotel. He was cycling hard, but he knew the perspiration was more to do with his nerves than with the exertion of riding his delivery bike. He had slept badly, his thoughts consumed with what to do about Commander Radcliffe. Eventually he had come up with a plan, but now, as he went to carry it out, he was aware of how easily it could go wrong.

He had slipped out of Hanlon's boarding house unseen, shutting from his mind how horrified Mrs Hanlon would be if she knew what he was doing. It was a quarter past eight now and Johnny had calculated carefully the time at which he wanted to arrive at the hotel. If he left it too late the rebels might already be in position, poised to go into action for their nine o'clock deadline. But if he acted too soon, Commander Radcliffe would discover the truth and realise that an operation was afoot. Johnny had calculated that about twenty past eight would be the perfect time to reach The Eastwood Hotel, and he accelerated now as he cycled along St Stephens Green.

Although it was early on a Sunday morning, the streets were surprisingly busy, with Tipperary supporters already on the move ahead of today's football match against Dublin in Croke Park. Johnny thought it was clever of the IRA to plan their move against the British agents for a day when town would be thronged with football supporters. The rebels could vanish into the crowds if the city was busy, and Johnny recognised good planning even as he tried to concentrate on his own mission.

He turned into Leeson Street, his heart beginning to thump as he approached The Eastwood Hotel. He tried breathing deeply to calm himself, then dismounted and leaned his bicycle against the lamppost as before. He looked around surreptitiously, but there was no sign of anybody staking out the premises. He paused briefly, getting up his nerve, then quickly mounted the steps into the hotel. He approached the desk with an air of urgency, hoping that his telegraph uniform would make his presence seem convincingly official. The friendly receptionist from last night was gone and in her place was a heavy-set man with horn-rimmed glasses.

'I've an urgent message for Wing Commander Radcliffe,' said Johnny confidently. 'Is he still in his room?'

'Yes.'

'What's the number?'

'You can't disturb a guest in his room. I'll ring him and tell him there's a telegram.'

'There isn't time for that. It's top priority, I've to give it to him in person.'

Johnny saw the man hesitate. 'I don't know. We don't normally—'

'This is life and death!' said Johnny cutting him short. 'His daughter is seriously ill. Just tell me the room number!'

'All right, all right. Room Seven. First floor.'

'Thank you,' said Johnny, already moving for the stairs.

He ascended two steps at a time then turned right into a carpeted corridor. He continued until he came to a door with seven on it. He had planned carefully what to do next, and he knocked on the door briskly, but not so loudly as to alarm other guests.

There was no immediate answer, and Johnny prayed that Radcliffe wasn't a heavy sleeper. *Come on*, he thought. He resisted the urge to knock again too soon, knowing that it was crucial to get

Stella's father out without alerting his officer friends. Just when Johnny was tempted to knock again he heard the lock being undone.

The door swung open and Commander Radcliffe stood in the doorway with a towel in his hand and his shirt collar undone.

'Johnny!' he said. 'What on earth are—'

'It's Stella!' cried Johnny. 'She's taken ill. You need to get to Balbriggan!'

'What?'

'She's really sick. Dr Foley said it's urgent, and you need to get to Balbriggan straight away.'

'Oh my God!'

Johnny felt bad about lying when he saw Radcliff's distress, but he pressed on. 'Have you got a car, Commander?'

'Yes, it's parked in Fitzwilliam Square.'

'Better leave everything here and make for the car.'

'Of course.'

Radcliffe threw down the towel, then grabbed his tie and jacket. He scooped up a wallet and a set of keys, then made for the door.

'What…what happened her, Johnny?'

'I don't know. But I'm sorry to be the bearer of bad news.'

Radcliffe closed the room door, and they made for the stairs.

'Why don't you just get to the car, and I'll stay back and send word that you're on your way?' said Johnny.

'Fine,' cried Radcliffe, descending at speed with Johnny at his hells. He paused briefly at the bottom and turned around. 'Thank you, Johnny. Thank you very much.' Before Johnny could answer Radcliffe nodded, then quickly made for the front door and exited to the street.

Johnny lowered his head into his hands, relieved that he may have saved the life of his friend's father. He stood there a moment, allowing his heartbeat to slow down, then he slung his satchel over his shoulder and walked swiftly out of The Eastwood Hotel.

Alice stopped dead in the lobby of the Mill. She and Stella were carrying their hockey gear, but both girls lowered their sticks as Commander Radcliffe burst in the door.

'Stella!' he cried crossing to her. 'What's…what's happened?!'

Alice had never seen her friend's father so wild-eyed, and Stella looked at him with equal bemusement.

'What's wrong, Dad?' she asked.

'Are you…are you all right?'

'Yes, I'm fine'

'Oh my God, Stella, I feared for your life!' He took her in his arms and hugged her, kissing her forehead.

Alice watched in amazement. Commander Radcliffe was a devoted father, but not normally given to public displays of affection, and Alice was intrigued to know what had brought this on.

'You feared for my life?' said Stella when her father released her from his embrace.

'Yes, I was told you were really ill.'

'What?'

'That Doctor Foley was treating you.'

'I haven't seen Doctor Foley in over a week. Who…who said this?'

Alice could see that Commander Radcliffe was totally perplexed.

'I…I thought the message was *from* Doctor Foley,' he said.

'But who delivered it?' persisted Stella.

'Johnny. Johnny Dunne.'

'Johnny? That…that makes no sense,' said Stella.

Alice was shocked too, and she struggled to make sense of it. To do such an odd thing, Johnny must have had a good reason. Could he possibly have lured Commander Radcliffe here on the orders of the IRA? No sooner had Alice thought it than she felt ashamed. Johnny was honourable, and he would never use his friendship with Stella to set up her father. So what was he up to?

'Johnny was adamant I get to you as soon as possible.'

'I've no idea why he'd do that,' said Stella.

'If it's some kind of practical joke, it's extremely ill-judged,' said Commander Radcliffe angrily. 'I'll see to it that he's dismissed.'

'He wouldn't do that as a joke, Dad.'

'Then what was he at?'

'We don't know, Commander,' said Alice. 'But please, don't do anything to have him sacked till we find out what's going on.'

'Very well. When did you last speak to him?'

'The day of Granddad's mass,' answered Stella, as the telephone on the reception desk behind them began to ring.

'Neither of us has seen him since then,' added Alice. *No need to reveal that Johnny had written and told them of the developments with his mother*, she thought, *that was a separate matter.*

'Telephone call for you, Commander,' said the receptionist.

'Really? Who is it?'

'Army Headquarters. They said it's urgent.'

Alice listened intrigued as Stella's father crossed to the desk and took up the telephone.

'Wing Commander Radcliffe speaking,' he said.

There was a long pause, but despite straining her ears, Alice couldn't hear what was being said done the telephone line

'God Almighty!' said Radcliffe, his face blanching as he gripped the telephone. He listened for another moment, then spoke again. 'What locations, sir?' He listened before raising another question. 'And at The Eastwood Hotel, was Lt. Colonel Jennings...?'

Alice looked at his face hoping for some clue, but his expression was stony. 'Yes, of course,' he said finally, 'I'll drove straight back to Headquarters. Thank you, sir.'

He put down the telephone, then turned to face Alice and Stella.

'What's going on? Dad?'

'British officers have been assassinated all over Dublin. At nine this morning IRA gunmen raided hotels and houses and shot unarmed officers.'

Alice was taken aback but she tried to think clearly. 'How... how many people have been shot?'

'There could be as many as twenty. There's a lot of confusion, but at least a dozen are dead for sure.'

'Oh, God,' said Stella. 'And...and The Eastwood Hotel where you stayed, Dad,' she continued tentatively. 'Was that attacked?'

He nodded.

'You could have been killed!'

'Yes...'

'Was...was your friend shot?'

'They haven't found a body for Lt. Colonel Jennings, so we're hoping for the best. It's all pretty chaotic.'

Suddenly it made sense to Alice. Johnny hadn't been acting *for* the IRA in going to The Eastwood Hotel. He'd protected Stella's father *from* them.

'So Johnny's story about me being sick,' said Stella as the truth appeared to dawn on her too, 'that was to get you out. He probably saved your life.'

Commander Radcliffe considered for a moment then nodded. 'So it seems.' He looked thoughtful, then turned his gaze back to the girls. 'But how did he know I was there? And more importantly, how did he know the attack was coming?'

'Maybe...maybe he overheard something?' said Stella. Even to Alice it sounded unconvincing, and she wasn't surprised when Commander Radcliffe shook his head.

'That's hardly likely,' he said.

Alice felt that she needed to deflect him from the truth of Johnny's situation. 'Maybe...maybe someone else sent him with that message. Johnny could have believed Stella really was sick.'

'Possibly. But if someone sent him, that person was close enough to the IRA to know their plans. How was Johnny involved with someone like that?'

Neither of the girls had a ready answer and Commander Radcliffe looked around. 'Where's Mom, Stella?'

'In my room. She's having a lie-on.'

'I'll have a quick word before I leave.'

'What's going to happen, Dad?'

He turned back to her and paused. 'There'll be a price to pay for what the IRA did,' he answered grimly. 'And I worry, I seriously worry, for the people who'll end up paying it.'

Alice watched him walk away. She was pleased that Johnny had saved the life of her friend's father, and sorry for the officers who had been shot in cold blood. Mostly though she was worried for Johnny, and she hoped fervently that he wouldn't be one of those who paid for today's events.

CHAPTER TWENTY-ONE

'We need to get you out of Dublin tonight, Johnny,' said Mrs Hanlon.

'That wasn't the plan,' he protested.

'The plan has changed!' she snapped.

Johnny was taken aback by her rare loss of composure.

'Sorry,' she said, raising a hand in apology. 'There's just so much going on.'

There was no denying that, thought Johnny, as he tried to marshal his thoughts. They were in Mrs Hanlon's sitting room, the gloom of a November dusk relieved by soft lighting and a roaring fire in the grate. Over the course of the day Johnny's emotions had been in turmoil. He had been hugely relieved to get Stella's father out of harm's way, and he knew now that his fears had been well founded, and that Commander Radcliffe could well have been shot as a fellow British officer by the men sent to execute Lt. Colonel Jennings. Johnny had been excited that Michael Collins's men had struck a stunning blow against British Intelligence. But he was also disturbed by the idea of unarmed agents being shot in cold blood, and he was uncomfortably aware that he had played a part in confirming the locations of some of the victims. He had accepted Mrs Hanlon's argument that Collins had struck the enemy before they could strike him, but he had still felt uneasy.

Then had come the devastating news that police, Auxiliaries and British troops had raided Croke Park during the Dublin versus Tipperary match. Johnny had expected some form of reprisals for the executions of the British agents, but he had been horrified to hear that the raiding party had opened fire on the crowd at the match, causing the deaths of fourteen spectators. Johnny knew it must have been a nightmare, with screaming spectators running in panic as the dead and wounded fell to the ground.

Nevertheless, Mrs Hanlon claimed that Collins had devastated British Intelligence in Ireland, with surviving agents scurrying to the safety of Dublin Castle. Johnny, though, felt that the deaths of fourteen innocent civilians was a high price to pay, and he was sickened that the authorities would lash out so indiscriminately. And if all that wasn't enough, now Mrs Hanlon was ordering him out of Dublin.

'Why can't I stay here?' he asked.

'It's not safe. If they can mow down football supporters, God knows where the backlash will end. Dick McKee and Peadar Clancy have been arrested, and there'll be more raids, and road-blocks, and checkpoints. And if they raid here as part of a crack-down they'll find out you lived here. Much better that you're gone if that happens.'

'But you're not going to leave, are you?'

'This is my home, so I'll brazen it out. But you've already said your mother wants you to live with her. Take her up on it, Johnny. Go to Scotland with her, you've more than done your bit for the cause.'

Part of Johnny resented the idea of fleeing the country, yet he knew that Mrs Hanlon was making sense. 'Supposing…supposing I do that. How do I get out of Dublin? You said there'll be road-blocks and checkpoints. If they're that much on the warpath, how do I get through the net?'

'It won't be easy. But I have an idea that I think will work.'

Johnny looked at her challengingly. Her steely blue eye held his gaze, however, and on instinct he decided to trust her. 'OK,' he said, 'tell me about it.'

'What a dreadful day,' said Mrs Goodman as she and Alice walked down the aisle of the parish church in Balbriggan, along-side Stella and Mrs Radcliffe. They had attended Benediction, the air heavy with incense while the organist played '*Tantum Ergo*' as the congregation prayed for the souls of all those killed earlier. Now the cold of November caused Stella to shiver as they stepped out into the night air.

'I wish it would all just stop,' she said.

'It won't though, will it?' said Alice. 'Killing those people in Croke Park was awful. It'll only make things worse.'

Stella hoped that this wouldn't be the case. Her father had reported to Army Headquarters, but she told herself that the government response to the IRA executions wouldn't involve much use of the RAF.

'I pray you're wrong, Alice,' said Mrs Radcliffe. 'Surely sense will prevail eventually.'

'We haven't seen much sense so far,' said Mrs Goodman as they passed out the gate of the church grounds and headed back towards the Mill. 'But maybe our prayers well be answered in time.'

'In a way they already have,' said Stella. 'Dad had a miraculous escape this morning.'

'Indeed,' said Mrs Goodman. 'But I'd like to know what Johnny Dunne was up to.'

'Whatever it was, he probably saved Dad's life,' answered Stella.

'For which we're greatly relieved. But his presence there…it suggests involvement.'

'Maybe he just heard something on the grapevine, Mam,' said Alice.

'Or maybe he played a part. I always suspected him of rebel sympathies. And I know it's a horrible thought, but perhaps he'd some link to this morning's killings. Maybe we should report it to the police.'

Stella immediately turned to her friend's mother. 'Don't do that, Mrs Goodman. Please.'

'Why not?'

'Because if he was involved – and I'm not saying he was – but if he was involved some way, we're even more in his debt. It would have taken huge courage to go against everyone on his own side, everything he believed in, to save Dad.'

'I…I hadn't thought of it that way,' said Mrs Goodman.

Stella looked at her appealingly. 'There's been enough trouble for one day. Please. Don't add to it by setting the police on Johnny.'

Mrs Goodman looked thoughtful, then nodded her head. 'All right. Maybe it's best to leave well enough alone for now.'

'Thank you,' said Stella. She sensed that the subject might not be closed permanently, but for now she had bought Johnny some time. Relieved by the thought, she linked arms with Alice and walked back towards the warmth of the Mill.

'Connecting you now, caller,' said the operator.

'Thank you,' answered Johnny, his pulses starting to throb. A lot depended on the outcome of this call, and if he didn't get his message away now he wouldn't get another chance tonight. He was in Mrs Hanlon's private parlour, his suitcase containing his dismantled clarinet at his feet, in preparation for his escape bid from Dublin.

He had already tried to contact his mother, ringing the chemist's shop in Athlone only to be told that she was out. The chemist had been pleasant and had offered to take a message, but what was there to say? *I'm Norah's son, and it's vital I contact her so we can flee the country?*

Johnny had thanked him and said he would try to make contact later. Now he waited anxiously as the telephone operator put him through on what he knew would be his final call.

'Mill Hotel,' came a voice down the line.

'Hello, could I speak to Alice, please?'

'Is that...is that Johnny?'

'Yes. Hello, Miss Hopkins,' he answered, recognising the voice of the receptionist.

'How are you, Johnny?'

'I'm fine thanks,' he answered, trying not to sound impatient. 'Is Alice there, I've an important message for her?'

'I'm sorry, Johnny, they all went to the church for Benediction.'

Johnny felt a surge of frustration, knowing that the Goodman's didn't normally go to Benediction on Sunday nights.

'I think there were going to be special prayers for all the people who were killed today,' said Miss Hopkins.

'Right.'

'They shouldn't be too much longer though. Can I pass on the message when they get in?'

Johnny wracked his brains, but couldn't think of any way to word his message that wouldn't give away information that should be kept secret.

'No it's...it's OK, Miss Hopkins.'

'You could try ringing her later. Or can I get her to contact you.'

'No. Thank you, but I have to leave in a couple of minutes.'

'Too bad. Though if you want – oh, wait now. She's coming in, Johnny. Hang on a minute and I'll put her on the line.'

Johnny felt his spirits soar. 'Thanks, Miss H. And do me a favour, will you, and keep it discreet. I don't want anyone else to know I've rung her.'

'All right, Johnny. Hold on.'

Johnny waited, then a moment later he heard the sound of Alice's voice.

'Hello?' she said.

'Hello, Alice, it's Johnny. Can you talk, or is your mam beside you?'

'I can talk. Mam is doing supper for Stella and Mrs Radcliffe. It's good to hear from you, Johnny.'

'Thanks.'

'And I know what you did this morning. That was really brave. Are you…are you OK?'

'I'm fine. But I have to get out of the country. I can't go into all the details because I've to leave in a couple of minutes.'

'All right.'

'Alice, I need you to do me a big favour.'

'Anything.'

'Can you ring my mother for me? It's Norah Dunne at Athlone 3423. '

'Norah Dunne, Athlone 3423. Got that,' said Alice.

'She's not there now, but she should be back.'

'OK, I'll ring in a while.'

'Thanks, Alice, it's vital I get a message to her.'

'Don't worry, I'll keep ringing till I get her. All night if need be.'

'You're a star, Alice.'

'So what do I tell her.'

'That I'm on for Scotland. But everything has to be brought forward because of what happened today. And can she meet me tomorrow?'

'That's moving fast.'

'It has to be this way.'

'All right. Where's she to meet you?'

'Balbriggan. No one there knows her. And we can get the train to Belfast and then the ferry to Scotland.'

'Is it not risky for you to come here where people will recognise you?'

'It's the last place they'd expect me to go. And I know it like the back of my hand so I'll be able to lie low.'

'Let me know when you get here,' said Alice. 'I'll get your mother a room in the Mill, and myself and Stella will help any way we can.'

'OK. And thanks, Alice, I'm really grateful.'

'Don't worry about that. Just get here safely.'

'I'll try. I'll talk to you tomorrow, I hope.'

'Till tomorrow then.'

Johnny hung up the phone. Then he picked up his suitcase and made for the door.

'I want you to look me in the eye, Stella,' said her mother.

They had entered Stella's bedroom in the Mill, having finished supper with the Goodmans, and Stella had anticipated that this moment might arise. She turned reluctantly and looked at her mother.

'Johnny Dunne…he's directly involved with the rebels, isn't he?'

Stella hesitated then nodded. 'Yes. But, Mom, he's involved in the same way that Dad is involved. He sees it as his duty.'

'For goodness sake! It's not the same thing, Stella. The authorities will crack down hard. He could end up in huge trouble.'

'I hope not. And I won't tell on him. He swore me to secrecy, Mom.'

'He swore you to secrecy? Against your own family?'

'It wasn't against my family. I've *always* fought Dad's corner. Even when the Tans and Auxies were turning people against the British, I stood up for Dad. And you weren't here, Mom. No blame – I know you had to nurse Granddad. But I needed a friend, and Johnny was a great friend. He was the first person here who got me to talk about what happened George. He helped make me see I shouldn't keep blaming myself. That was a huge thing for me.' Stella sensed that she was swaying her mother and she decided to go for broke. 'And he probably saved Dad's life this morning. You can't deny that.'

'I'm not…'

'Then please, Mom, don't take against him. Both sides did awful things today. But making one fourteen-year-old pay for it isn't right. If they come asking questions, don't inform on him.' Stella reached out and took her mother's hand. 'Please, Mom, I'm begging you.'

Johnny gripped his mug of cocoa in both hands, sipping the warm drink to counteract the falling temperature. Frost-covered trees glinted in the moonlight as he glided over the icy waters of the Royal Canal. He was sitting in the cabin of a long barge, its hold filled with a cargo of brandy for delivery to Mullingar.

Johnny thought it was smart of Mrs Hanlon to call in a favour with a rebel bargeman to smuggle him out of Dublin. After a day of murder and mayhem there would be cordons and checkpoints on the city's roads. The barge, however, had attracted little attention as it rose through a series of locks on its way towards the city's outskirts. At every lock Johnny had held his suitcase in hand, ready to flee the vessel should it be inspected. But no one had been suspicious of a working barge, and now he tried to relax as the vessel cruised towards the outlying village of Blanchardstown.

The plan was that Johnny would sleep on board when it stopped for the night in the town of Maynooth. Then first thing in the morning he would resume this journey to Balbriggan to rendezvous with his mother. *Assuming that Alice could contact her. Assuming, too, that she was willing to drop everything and take him with her to Scotland.* Still, all of that was out of his hands for now; his priority was to get away from Dublin.

Just before he had left, Mrs Hanlon had heard disturbing news. Two IRA volunteers, Peadar Clancy and Dick McKee, and their friend Conor Clune, who had been arrested the previous night, had been killed in custody. The official story was that they were shot while trying to escape, but Mrs Hanlon was convinced that it was another reprisal for this morning's killings of British intelligence officers.

With the backlash becoming ever more brutal, Johnny feared for Mrs Hanlon herself, *How long could it be before somebody being interrogated mentioned her name?* And if Mrs Hanlon was interrogated might she break down and give Johnny's name? He prayed that wouldn't happen, then his musings were cut short as he heard a change in the engine's sound.

The steady chug-chugging dropped in volume as the barge began to slow down. Johnny immediately moved to the door of the darkened cabin and quietly opened it. Ahead in the moonlight he could see the outline of a large mill, adjacent to the next lock. Johnny knew that the previous lock had been Lock Eleven, so this would be the Twelfth Lock, at the outskirts of Blanchardstown.

Johnny looked behind him and saw the tillerman steering the slowing craft towards the quay.

One of the bargemen jumped ashore, a rope in one hand and a key for the lock in the other. Just as the moon went behind a cloud, Johnny glimpsed two tall figures approaching the bargemen. There was a gas lamp at the side of the quay, but outside of its limited yellow halo of light, Johnny couldn't see the two men.

'Evening, sir,' said one of them, in a lilting Cork accent.

'Evening, officer,' answered the bargeman.

Johnny tried to keep his nerves under control. There had been no police presence at any of other locks, and it would be awful to come close to escaping only to be caught now.

'Where are you coming from?' asked the policeman.

'Spencer Dock. Bringing a cargo of brandy to Mullingar.'

'Brandy, is it?' said the second officer, who also had a country accent. 'I hope you haven't been sampling the cargo?'

Johnny felt a tiny sliver of relief. The men didn't seem hostile, and their accents suggested Royal Irish Constabulary, rather than Tans or Auxies.

'Rather have a few pints in Maynooth than a keg full of brandy!' said the bargeman.

Johnny was impressed by his cool demeanour, and he hoped the policemen would be swayed by his relaxed tone.

'Fair enough,' said the policeman easily.

Johnny sensed that things were going to be all right, and he unclenched his hand, which had been gripping his suitcase.

'Look, we won't delay you,' said the first policeman.

'Thanks, officer.'

'But with all that's happened today, we need to do a quick check on your crew and cargo.'

Johnny's mouth went dry. It had been agreed that if he were caught the bargemen would deny all knowledge of him and claim he was a stowaway. But although that might well get them off the hook, it would spell disaster for Johnny.

Without hesitating, he grasped his suit case, ducked low and made for the side of the vessel. With the moon behind the cloud the night was dark, and if he was quiet he might get away before the RIC men spotted him.

As if reading his intentions, and seeking to buy him time, the bargeman spoke up.

'Do we really have to do that, officer? Everything is in order, and it's a freezing night. We just want to be on our way.'

'The sooner we get this done the sooner we can all get warm again,' answered the policeman.

Johnny could barely make out the frosty quayside in the dark, but every second counted, and with his suitcase in hand he jumped from the side of the barge.

He landed awkwardly, dropping the suitcase. Immediately he rose to his feet again, grabbing the handle of the case, but the noise had been heard and the first policeman called out.

'Who's that? Show yourself!'

Johnny knew that the RIC were armed, and if he didn't surrender he might end up getting shot. But it was dark, and the policeman had heard him rather than seen him. If he ran for it now he might get away. He hesitated for half a second, terrified of getting a bullet in the back, but terrified too of being captured and interrogated.

He saw a shadow in the gaslight, as the policeman moved forward, then suddenly his mind was made up and he sprinted in the opposite direction.

'Stop! Stop in the name of the law!' cried the policeman.

But Johnny was committed now, and he ran flat out, praying he wouldn't lose his balance on the frosty ground. He sprinted back along the towpath. Immediately he heard the sound of a police whistle being blown and he felt a sudden sense of exhilaration. *A policeman blowing a whistle was summoning help – which was much better than a policeman shooting at him.* Buoyed by the thought, he upped his speed, leaving the barge behind and vanishing into the night.

Alice tip-toed out of her bedroom, taking care not to wake her mother in the adjoining room. She avoided the slightly creaky floor board in the living room floor, then gently opened the door. She paused a moment, listening to ensure that there was no sound coming from Mam's room. Her mother tended to go to bed early and sleep soundly, and to Alice's relief all was quiet. She stepped out, softly closing the door. She tightened her dressing gown and made for the hotel office. There was a telephone in their private quarters, but Alice couldn't let Mam know that she was making calls on Johnny's behalf.

She reached the end of the corridor and was glad to see that the reception desk was unmanned. Moving behind the desk, she entered the office, closed the door and seated herself beside the telephone. So far she had failed to contact Johnny's mother, with the chemist in Athlone answering her call and explaining that Norah Dunne had gone out. He wasn't sure what time she would be back, and he had offered to ask Miss Dunne to return the call. Alice had declined and said she would call back in an hour.

That call had been unsuccessful too, and Alice was anxious now as she prepared to ring again. How many times could she call before the chemist lost patience with her? And what if Johnny's mother didn't come home tonight, but stayed with friends? Alice stopped and took a deep breath, knowing that she had to calm herself. She placed the call with the operator, then found that she was biting her lip as the she heard the telephone ringing at the other end. She breathed deeply again, then her hopes rose when the call was answered by a woman.

'Hello, would that be Norah Dunne, please?'

'Yes, this is Norah Dunne. Are you the girl who was looking for me?'

'Yes. My name is Alice Goodman. I'm a friend of Johnny's.'

'I know who you are, Alice. Is Johnny all right?'

Alice could hear the anxiety in the woman's voice. She realised how worrying it must have been for Johnny's mother to have missed a series of calls on a day when so many people had been killed and injured.

'It's OK, Johnny hasn't been hurt.'

'Thank God for that!'

'But he needs to get out of Ireland. He said you were leaving for Scotland, and could he come with you?'

'Yes, of course. I'd planned to go next weekend.'

'Can you bring that forward? Johnny needs to leave right away.'

'Is he…is he in danger?'

'He didn't go into details. But he wouldn't be doing this unless he had to. I know it's huge thing to ask, but…could you drop everything and go tomorrow?'

Alice had worried that this might not be possible, but Norah Dunne's answer gladdened her heart.

'I'll go tonight if need be,' she said simply.

'That's…that's just brilliant, Miss Dunne. But the plan is for you both to meet up tomorrow in Balbriggan.'

'OK, I'll pack tonight. I'll explain that for family reasons my plans have changed, and get the first train in the morning.'

'Perfect.'

'What time do we meet and where?'

'I don't know how Johnny plans to get out of Dublin, or how long it might take him to get here. The best thing is if you come to the Mill Hotel and check in. I'll make a booking for you now. I'll do it in the name of Miss Dunne. No one here will connect that with Johnny.'

'Thank you, Alice. I'm…I'm very grateful.'

'You're fine. It's great that you can do this.'

'He's my son. I'd do anything for him.'

Alice felt a sudden affection for this woman that she had never met. 'Grand. I'll see you tomorrow, Miss Dunne. Safe journey.'

'I'll see you tomorrow, Alice. God bless.'

Alice hung up, then sat back in the chair, suddenly spent. She felt enormously relieved to have carried out Johnny's wish and to have contacted his mother. But that would count for nothing if he was caught before he could reach Balbriggan. She sat unmoving for a moment, praying that her friend would be all right. Then she told herself that there was no more she could do tonight, and she rose resignedly and started back towards her room.

Johnny watched the flames dancing in the firelight and he snuggled deeper into the folds of his overcoat, glad to be in out of the frosty night air. He had run blindly at first to evade the policemen at the Twelfth Lock, then when he was confident that he had left them behind he had made his way into a heavily wooded estate. The moon had come out again, allowing him to a follow a trail, and the gaunt, leafless trees had looked ghostly in the moonlight, their branches glistening with frost. Johnny, however, had been oblivious to the wintry beauty of the scene, and conscious that he needed to find shelter. He didn't know how cold it had to get for someone to die of exposure, but he reckoned that sleeping rough on a freezing night was a bad idea.

He had hoped to find a barn or perhaps a deserted cottage, but instead had eventually come across a wooden cabin deep in the woods. Its door had been unlocked but stiff, and Johnny had had to use his shoulder to force an entry. Inside it was draughty and barely furnished, with just a couple of rickety chairs. But there were matches by the fireside, kindling in the grate, and neatly stacked chopped logs, and Johnny gave silent thanks to the estate workers who obviously used it as an occasional base.

Johnny had thought twice about lighting the fire, not wanting to draw attention. But he needed to get warm, and he had reasoned that this late at night and in such an isolated spot nobody was likely to come across the cabin.

Now he was stretched out before the fire, sitting in one chair with his feet resting on the other and with his overcoat wrapped tightly around him. He found his thoughts drifting as the warmth of the fire and sheer exhaustion made him sleepy. It had been an incredibly eventful day, what with the drama of warning Commander Radcliffe, the killings of the British agents, the reprisals at Croke Park, and his own escape from the police. To think about it too much was overwhelming, and there was no guarantee that Alice had reached his mother or that she could suddenly leave Athlone to flee with him to Scotland. And what would happen if Mrs Hanlon was arrested? Or if he himself got picked up tomorrow by the police, or even worse, by the Tans?

It was easy to imagine everything spiralling out of control, but with an effort he forced himself to simply take one thing at a time. Then tiredness overtook him, and warmed by the gently crackling fire, he succumbed to a deep, dreamless sleep.

CHAPTER TWENTY-TWO

Johnny woke with a start. Hazy early morning sunlight had brightened the interior of the cabin, however it wasn't the light that had woken him but rather the sound of a man's voice.

'Well, well, what have we got here?'

Johnny's heart quickened as he came to, and took in his surroundings.

The cabin interior looked ramshackle in the morning light, but Johnny's attention was focussed on the man who stood before him, a shotgun casually draped over his arm. His clothes and his accent didn't indicate a landowner. But he seemed sure of himself, and Johnny feared that he had been caught by a gamekeeper.

He swung his legs down from the chair and rose to his feet a little unsteadily, his muscles stiff from his awkward sleeping position.

The man with the shotgun was short and stocky with slightly bloodshot eyes that nonetheless seemed watchful.

'I didn't mean any harm,' said Johnny. 'I...I got lost last night and I needed somewhere to get in out of the cold.'

'Is that a fact?' said the man.

His tone sounded lightly mocking, but not openly aggressive.

'You know, of course, you're trespassing?' he added.

Johnny didn't answer at once. The man had left the door of the cabin open behind him. If Johnny tripped him up, might he grab the suitcase and make his escape out the door? Or would it be suicidal to grapple with a man armed with a shotgun?

'I didn't mean to trespass,' answered Johnny, wanting to buy time while he figured out what to do. 'But I lost my bearings, and I needed shelter.'

'Really? And why was a kid like you travelling alone?'

'I was going to meet my mother.'

'Late at night, in the middle of the countryside?'

'She...she works in the evening. I was going to meet her when she finished her shift,' answered Johnny. The man said nothing, but he looked thoughtful, as though weighing up what he might do. Johnny also weighed up his options and thought again about making for the door. It was only feet away, but the man seemed alert and was standing directly in his way.

'I hope your mother doesn't work in Blanchardstown, does she?' said the man.

'No.'

'Because there was an incident there last night. The police are looking for someone who ran off.'

Johnny swallowed hard, but tried to keep his face impassive.

The man looked Johnny directly in the eye. 'If I was that person, I'd give Blanchardstown a wide berth.'

Johnny held his gaze, realising with a surge of joy that he was being helped. 'Right,' he said.

The man turned sideways and indicated the track outside the cabin door. 'That trail eventually leads to the Ballycoolin Road. Anyone taking that route would bypass Blanchardstown.'

'That sounds like a good plan.'

'After yesterday in Croke Park the police have a nerve to be showing their faces at all.'

'Yeah, it's awful what was done,' said Johnny.

'I wouldn't like to see anyone else becoming their victim. You be careful, son.'

'Don't worry, I will,' said Johnny, taking up his suitcase.

'I won't ask you where you're going, better I don't know. But good luck to you,' said the man, offering his hand.

'Thanks, Mister,' answered Johnny. He reached out and shook the man's hand, then he nodded in farewell, stepped out the door and started off along the frost-covered trail.

'What's wrong, Alice?'

Alice gripped the side of the breakfast table and grimaced, then turned to her mother. 'Sorry, Mam, I just got a cramp.'

Her mother looked concerned. 'Are you all right?'

'I don't feel great. It must be something I ate. I was sick earlier.'

'You should have told me.'

'I didn't want to make a fuss.'

'Maybe you shouldn't have a full breakfast. Plain toast might help to settle your stomach.'

'Yes, I feel…I feel pretty queasy.'

'You poor lamb,' said her mother, reaching out and squeezing her hand.

'I'm sure it will pass eventually,' said Alice. No sooner had she said the words than she gripped the table and grimaced again.

'It might be best, love, if you stayed home from school,' suggested her mother.

On hearing the words Alice felt elated, but she made sure not to show it. Instead she nodded. 'Yes, maybe I should.' Although she had dressed in her school uniform to make it look convincing, she had never had any intention of going to classes today. With Johnny's mother due in Balbriggan and Johnny also en route she needed to be at the Mill to help them. But it was better that it seem like Mam's idea to stay home, and so she had faked the symptoms of her imaginary illness.

She looked now at Mam's concerned face and felt a pang of guilt. But telling a white lie about being sick was less important than getting Johnny safely out of the country. Assuming he *could* get safely to Scotland. And even that wasn't an attractive outcome when it would mean not seeing her friend again for God knows how long.

'Why don't you go and have a lie down?' suggested her mother, breaking Alice's reverie. 'I'll give Stella a note for Sister Mary. Go on now, I'll bring you in tea and toast on a tray.'

'Thanks Mam. You're the best!' Alice rose from her chair, kissed her mother on the cheek, then headed happily back towards her room.

Johnny knew that first impressions counted, and he adopted a confident stride as he approached Dunboyne train station. He was hungry, thirsty and tired, but to any casual observer he wanted to look like a well-dressed boy getting the train for Navan. It had been a long walk from the woods where he had slept – made longer by the need to bypass Blanchardstown. As he had walked the country lanes the quickly melting frost had sparkled in the morning sunshine. Johnny's spirits had lifted, then before reaching Dunboyne he had tidied himself up. Brushing down his overcoat and carefully wiping away the mud from his shoes, he had made sure that he looked smart, and it paid off now with nobody giving him a second glance as he approached the entrance to the station. There were several passengers ahead of him in the ticket hall but to Johnny's relief there was no sign of any policemen.

He took his place in the queue and slipped his hand into his pocket to have his money ready. His modest life savings were folded up inside his sock, but last night Mrs Hanlon had given him two ten shilling notes, and he intended to use one of them to buy his ticket. Johnny was grateful that she was such a painstaking planner, and this morning he had navigated by a map of Leinster that she had given him in case he had to flee the barge.

Now he got to the head of the queue, and nodded to the ticket seller, a plump, grey haired man with a slightly brusque manner.

'What can I get you?' asked the man.

'A single to Navan, please.'

The man didn't make eye contact, and Johnny was glad, wanting to stay as anonymous as possible. He paid for the ticket, knowing that when he got to Navan on the Midland Great Western railway he would have to change for the Great Northern line to take him to Drogheda, after which he would loop back south until he reached Balbriggan. It was a roundabout way of getting to his destination. But that actually worked for him, in that nobody was likely to predict his taking such a circuitous route. *But the Tans or Auxies could still do a spot check on one of the trains.* Well, he would cross that bridge if he came to it.

Johnny took his ticket, then moved to the refreshment stand. He had had nothing since the cocoa the night before on the barge and his mouth began to water. *Don't suddenly stuff your face with food and drink,* he thought, knowing that it wasn't what a middle-class boy would do in public. Instead he ordered a glass of milk, a ham sandwich, and a bar of chocolate.

He slipped the chocolate bar into his pocket, then sat down on a bench and forced himself to eat the sandwich unhurriedly. He knew that it was unlikely that anyone was watching him, but his training by Mr O'Shea had ingrained in him the importance of never doing anything to attract attention.

Sipping his milk and munching his sandwich, he thought ahead to what might happen later today. He knew that if he could get to Balbriggan he could absolutely count on both Alice and Stella, the two best friends he had ever had. But would his mother be able to leave everything and travel there? And even if she did, and if they got away to Scotland, it would mean Johnny leaving behind his friends. It felt like there were too many issues to cope with and once more he decided to stop thinking about the future and just concentrate on what was happening now. He finished his milk and sandwich, treated himself to half the bar of chocolate, and then waited patiently until he heard the sound of a train whistle.

'Navan train, coming in,' said a bystander.

At last, thought Johnny, anxious to start the next phase of his journey. Then he rose, picked up his suitcase and headed out to the platform.

Stella ran along High Street eager to get to the Mill as soon as possible. Sister Mary put a high value on girls from the convent deporting themselves like ladies, but today Stella didn't care about the rules. She had to know if Johnny or his mother had reached Balbriggan safely.

Stella had waited until break time, then told her teacher that she was coming down with the same bug that had affected Alice. On a normal day the teacher might have suggested contacting Stella's mother, who had gone in to Dublin with Commander

Radcliffe. Nothing about today had been normal, however, with people stunned by the previous day's killings, and with special prayers being said for the many dead. Stella's teacher had allowed her to travel unescorted the short distance back to the Mill, and now she quickly entered the building and approached reception.

'Is Alice about?' she asked.

'In her room, Stella,' answered the receptionist.

'Thanks.' She quickly made her way down the corridor, then knocked on the door to the Goodman's private quarters.

A moment later Alice opened the door.

'Stella, come in.'

'Is your mam here?' asked Stella cautiously, stepping into the room.

'No, she had to go to Rush to meet a vegetable supplier. So, your plan worked?'

'Yeah, I waited a few hours, then got your bug. Has Johnny arrived?'

'Not yet.'

'And his mother?'

'No sign of her either.'

'God…'

'I wouldn't worry too much about her. When we spoke last night she was definitely on for it. With everything that's happened, though, there might be delays.'

'Maybe. And no word from Johnny?'

'No.'

'I wonder what's keeping him. I mean, he'd only to come from Dublin.'

'Who knows?' said Alice. 'He didn't tell me how they were smuggling him out. Maybe it was complicated.'

'Or maybe…I hate to sound negative, but maybe they couldn't get him out.'

'I really hope they did. But there's no way of knowing.'

Stella thought for a moment then looked at her friend. 'There is one way. We could ring the place where he lived.'

'But Johnny told us never to do that! He wasn't supposed to tell us *any* of what he was doing.'

'After yesterday, Alice, all the rules are out the window.'

Alice nodded. 'Yeah…you're right. OK, let's ring from here. You're better at thinking on your toes, do you want to speak to them?'

'All right,' agreed Stella.

She listened as her friend asked the operator to connect her to Hanlon's boarding house, then took the phone when the call was put through.

A deep man's voice answered. 'Hello?'

'Hello, may I speak to Mrs Hanlon, please?'

'Who is this?'

Stella paused briefly. 'Annie Keegan,' she answered, giving the name of the cook at her old school in Toronto. The man's English accent had Stella on extra alert, and the lie had come naturally.

'And what did you want with Mrs Hanlon?'

'Eh, I wanted to ask about accommodation. May I have a word?'

'Mrs Hanlon is in police custody.'

Stella was shocked, and she gripped the phone more tightly.

'Have you stayed here before?' asked the man.

'No.'

'So what's your connection to Mrs Hanlon?'

Time to end this call, thought Stella. 'I was recommended Hanlon's for lodgings. I'm sorry to hear of her problems, but thank you for telling me. Good day.' Stella hung up before the man could respond.

'What's wrong?' asked Alice.

'Mrs Hanlon has been arrested.'

'Oh God, no!'

'I think the man I spoke to was a Tan or an Auxie. And if they're still there, then maybe she was only arrested this morning.'

'So Johnny probably got away last night.'

'Let's hope so. But even if he did, when they check who else was living in the house they'll discover Johnny was. It can't be long till they trace him back to Balbriggan.'

Alice looked worried. 'How long would you say that would take?'

'I don't know.'

'Then the sooner Johnny and his mother get here the better.'

'Absolutely,' said Stella. 'I think it's just turned into a race against time.'

* * *

Johnny spotted the two policemen as he queued to buy his train ticket at Drogheda railway station. Their presence was frightening, but he forced himself to think clearly. The good news was that the station was busy, with lots of passengers waiting for the Dublin-bound train that was due in shortly. The bad news was that the RIC officers, their rifles slung on their shoulders, had positioned themselves out on the platform.

Johnny got to the head of the queue, nervously weighing up his options. He could turn away and forget about the train. But to walk from Drogheda to Balbriggan would take hours. And he might well be spotted by police walking along the main road carrying a suitcase.

'Yes, please?' said the ticket seller.

Johnny hesitated, then followed his instincts. 'Single to Balbriggan, please.'

He paid for the ticket, telling himself that someone who had run from a barge near Dublin the previous night was probably not a priority for the police in Drogheda. Then again, after the slaughter of yesterday – people were calling it Bloody Sunday – maybe all police officers would be extra vigilant.

Johnny heard the rumbling sound of an approaching engine, then there was a hiss of steam as the Dublin-bound train pulled in to the station and came to a stop. He picked up his suitcase and quickly scanned the other passengers who were preparing to board the train. Nearby there was a family group sorting out their luggage. Besides the parents, there were two girls in their late teens a boy of about fourteen. *Much better to appear part of a family group than to stand out a solo traveller,* Johnny decided, as he drew near and nodded to the boy.

'Heading down to Dublin?' said Johnny casually as he fell into step beside him.

'Yes, we were visiting my cousins.'

Johnny could see the policemen out of the corner of his eye, then he turned to face his companion.

'I hope your cousins are less of a pain than my cousins!' he said softly.

The boy laughed, and Johnny joined in as they passed the RIC men. One part of him half expected a sudden hand on his shoulder. But still chatting easily, they reached the carriage door unmolested. Hugely relieved, Johnny entered the train. In twenty minutes they would reach Balbriggan, and then would come the trickiest part of all. But for now he was still on schedule, and he stowed his suitcase, took a seat, and sat back comfortably, conserving his energy for what lay ahead.

Alice was startled by a sudden series of knocks on her bedroom door. She looked at Stella, then quickly crossed to the door and opened it.

'Miss Hopkins,' she said, excited to see the receptionist.

'She's here. You told me to tell you when the lady for room nine arrived.'

'Good,' said Alice calmly, not wanting Miss Hopkins to know how relieved she was that Johnny's mother had made it. 'Ask the porter, please, to bring her case up to room nine, and then if you wouldn't mind bringing Miss Dunne back down here to me and Stella.'

'Right away.'

'Thank you.'

Stella raised an eyebrow as Alice closed the door again. 'I thought we'd go to meet her.'

'Better not to draw attention in the lobby,' said Alice.

'Fair enough,' conceded Stella. 'One down, one to go,'

'Yeah, I wish Johnny would show up.'

'Knowing Johnny, he'll do everything humanly possible.'

'I know. I wonder…I wonder does his mother look like him? I'm dying to see her.'

'Me too.'

After a moment a gentle knock sounded on the door, and Alice looked at Stella. 'Time to find out.'

She opened the door to find a well-dressed woman with wavy brown hair and alert blue eyes. The woman looked younger than Alice had expected, but there was no doubting that she was Johnny's mother.

'Miss Dunne,' said Alice. 'Please, come in.'

The woman stepped into the room, a faint hint of sweet-smelling soap trailing in the air behind her.

'You're Alice, that I spoke to last night?' she said.

'Yes,' she answered, shaking hands, 'and this is my friend, Stella Radcliffe.'

Stella shook hands also, then Johnny's mother looked at them and smiled warmly.

'It's lovely to meet you, girls. Though I feel I know you already, Johnny has told me so much about you!'

She was well spoken with a soft midlands accent, and Alice found herself taking to her straight away. 'All good, I hope?' said Alice playfully.

'Ninety-nine point-nine percent,' said Miss Dunne with a grin, before her expression became more serious. 'So, has Johnny arrived?'

'Not yet. Would you like some tea while we're waiting?' offered Alice.

'Yes, that would be lovely, thanks.'

'Grand, but eh…just before I put on the kettle, there's something I need to tell you.'

'Oh?'

'Stella rang Hanlon's guesthouse where Johnny had been living. Mrs Hanlon has been arrested.'

'Oh dear.'

'It's probably just a matter of time till they find that Johnny lived there, but used to work here.'

'And then they'll come here?'

'I'd say so. We can't do much till Johnny arrives, so we may as well relax with a cup of tea. And if you'd like to freshen up you can go up to room nine.'

'But the Tans *could* already be on their way here,' said Stella.

'So once Johnny arrives, we need to make our move.'

'I think so,' said Alice.

Miss Dunne nodded decisively. 'Right. Then that's what we'll do.'

CHAPTER TWENTY-THREE

'Here's the money,' said Stella, handing over a bank-note.

Alice could see that her friend was trying to sound calm, but the excitement was evident in her voice. They were in the lobby of the Mill, and Stella had just come from room nine, where Johnny's mother was freshening up while she awaited his arrival.

'Great,' said Alice, taking the money and slipping it into the pocket of her overcoat. It had been Stella's idea to speed things up by buying train tickets for Belfast while they waited for Johnny. From Belfast, Johnny and his mother would get the ferry to Scotland, but Stella had pointed out that if the police arrived in Balbriggan in pursuit of Johnny it might be better if the ticket seller at the train station hadn't seen Miss Dunne purchasing tickets.

'OK, I won't be long' said Alice.

'Fine, I'll go back and wait with Miss Dunne.'

Alice crossed the lobby and exited into the street. Normally she loved crisp winter weather, but today the combination of blue sky and soft November sunshine was lost on her. Instead her senses were on alert for any sign of police activity as she made for the train station. Walking briskly, she passed the shells of several buildings that had been destroyed when the Tans had torched the town in September. Apart from the sight of the burnt-out ruins – which still angered Alice, even eight weeks later – everything seemed normal.

She reached the station and made for the ticket sales window. Although there were passengers here in the hall and in the waiting room, there was only one person in the queue ahead of her. Alice tried to curb her impatience as the woman bought her ticket, slowly taking out one coin after another from her purse to pay for it.

Finally, she finished the transaction, and Alice came face to face with the ticket seller. He was Larry McCaffrey, a local man in his late twenties who was friendly and outgoing. Alice would have preferred to buy the tickets from someone who didn't know her, but Larry greeted her by name.

''Morning, Alice, fit and well you're looking.'

'Good morning, Larry.'

'What can I get you?'

'Two single tickets for Belfast please.'

'Running away with your boyfriend, are you?' said Larry with a grin.

Alice forced herself to smile. 'Obliging a guest at the Mill,' she answered. 'One adult and one child, please,' she said, making her tone business-like as she handed over the pound note that Stella had been given by Miss Dunne.

She hoped Larry wouldn't waste what might be precious time with more ham-fisted jokes, and to her relief she realised that he had picked up on her tone.

'There you are,' he said, giving her the tickets and her change without further ado.

'Thanks, Larry,' she answered. Then she nodded in farewell, strode towards the door and started back towards the Mill.

Johnny felt his anxiety worsening as the train pulled in to Balbriggan station. He had tried to relax as the train travelled through the sun-dappled countryside, but the stark beauty of the winter landscape had passed in a blur as his worries mounted. Supposing there was a police checkpoint at Balbriggan station and he was questioned? Supposing Mr O'Shea and Mrs Hanlon had been picked up in the crackdown after the assassination of the British Intelligence agents? Or supposing his mother had been prevented from travelling from Athlone to Balbriggan? Could she even have had second thoughts about helping him escape to Scotland in the aftermath of all the killings yesterday? She had left him once before as a baby, supposing she left him once again now?

No sooner had Johnny thought this than he felt guilty. His mother had explained why she had put him up for adoption, and had apologised from the heart for all he had suffered in St Mary's. She was the one who had suggested a life together in Scotland, and he chided himself now for doubting her. Before he could think about it any further the train shuddered to a stop. Johnny took up his case and exited from the carriage, quickly scanning

225

the platform as he stepped out into the November air. There were no policemen about, however, and he quickly left the station and began walking towards the Mill Hotel. He walked at a good pace, but not so swiftly as to draw attention. He was about halfway there when he spotted the local surgeon, Doctor Foley, coming in his direction. Johnny had hoped to rendezvous with his mother without bumping into anyone who knew him. Could he cross to the other side of the street and avoid Dr Foley? No, he decided, that would look odd – better to act as though everything was normal.

'Doctor Foley,' he said in respectful greeting as they drew level.

'Johnny,' the surgeon replied, a note of surprise in his voice as he took in the suitcase. 'Coming back to work in the Mill?'

'No, I'm just breaking my journey on the way to Dublin,' answered Johnny, the lie tripping easily off his tongue.

'Ah. Be careful in Dublin, it seems to be in turmoil.'

'I will, thanks. Well, good day, Doctor Foley.'

'Good day, Johnny.'

He nodded politely and moved on. He knew that normally it would be someone of Doctor Foley's social standing who decided when to end an encounter. Today though he was in a hurry; if Doctor Foley found that a little strange, then too bad. Striding on before Foley could question him further, he soon came to the rear entrance of the Mill. Wanting to avoid attention, he went in through the back gate, crossed the yard and stepped through the rear door. The heated interior and the scent of food from the kitchen were reassuringly familiar, and Johnny followed the route that he had taken countless times before, bringing him to reception.

'Hello, Miss Hopkins,' he said.

'Johnny!' she answered.

'Is Norah Dunne here?'

'Yes, she's in room nine.'

Johnny felt a surge of relief.

'Alice and Stella are with her,' added Miss Hopkins with a lowered voice. 'They're waiting for you.'

'Are Alice and Stella not in school?'

'They've both upset stomachs. They're excused school.'

'Right,' said Johnny, trying to keep back a grin.

He left reception and took the stairs, then knocked on the door of room nine. Almost immediately the door opened, and there stood Alice, a huge smile on her face.

'Johnny! Thank God you made it!' she said.

She threw her arms around him, then ushered him into the room. Johnny's spirits soared to see the smiling faces of Stella and his mother. Stella reached him first, and like Alice, gave him a hug.

'We were so worried about you!'

'*I* was worried about me!' answered Johnny playfully.

His mother approached, and when he turned to her, Johnny could see that she had tears in her eyes. He suddenly felt a lump in his own throat, but tried to keep his emotions in check. 'Mam,' he said.

'Johnny.' she replied. Without another word she took him in

her arms.

After all that he had been through, Johnny found comfort in her embrace, then after a moment they separated.

'I hate being the bearer of bad news,' said Stella hesitantly. 'But there's something you need to know, Johnny.'

'What's that?'

'I tried to ring you in Dublin. But the police answered the phone. Mrs Hanlon has been arrested.'

Johnny felt his mouth going dry. 'God…' he said. 'And…and what about Mr O'Shea?'

'I don't know about him,' answered Stella. 'But the thing is, they're likely to trace you back to the Mill.'

'We all reckon it's just a matter of time till the Tans show up,' said Alice. 'I've bought train tickets. We think you and your mam should go while the going is good.'

'Right.'

'But before we do, I was telling the girls about my idea to boost our chances,' said his mother.

'Oh? What's that?'

His mother looked mysterious. 'Step into the bathroom, and I'll show you.'

'Remember the book we got in the library about magic tricks?' said Stella.

'Yes,' answered Alice.

Stella could see that her friend was bemused by her choice of topic. They were waiting for Johnny and his mother to finish in the bathroom, and Stella had been thinking about how to boost their chances of leaving Ireland undetected. '*Misdirection* was the big thing in that book,' she said. 'If a magician doesn't want you to see what his left hand is doing, he'll draw your attention to his right hand.'

'Yes, I know what misdirection is.'

'I think we should try and do a bit of that for Johnny and his mam.'

'How?'

'By thinking the way the police might think, and then misguiding them. I mean, this could all be a storm in a teacup, and maybe they're not looking for Johnny at all.'

'But if they *are*, we try to fool them?'

'Yes. If you were a republican fleeing the country, Alice, where would you make for?'

'Probably…America. Lots of Irish sympathisers there.'

'Exactly. So if the Tans *do* get on Johnny's trail, it would be good to make them think he's gone there instead of Scotland.'

'How do we do that?'

'I don't know yet, but we can be thinking about it. Meanwhile I have fruit and chocolate in my room. If I give them that they won't have to buy stuff. The fewer people they show their faces to the better, till they're out of the country.

'Yes, that makes sense.'

'OK, I'll slip down and get the grub. Won't be a minute.'

Stella left the room and went quickly down the stairs, then entered her own room and crossed to the fruit bowl. She took apples and bananas, and slipped them into a brown paper bag, before adding a large bar of chocolate that she had been saving for after hockey training. Pleased with her forward thinking, she locked the door after her and started back towards room nine.

She crossed the edge of the lobby and was about to climb the stairs when she saw a Crossley tender pulling to a halt outside the hotel. To her dismay she saw heavily armed Tans spilling out of the vehicle. She paused a moment, hoping against hope that the Mill wasn't their destination. Then she saw the leading Tan making for the entrance. Without wasting another moment she turned on her heel and made for room nine, taking the stairs at speed.

'When was the last time you saw Johnny Dunne?' demanded the Tan.

He spoke with a thick Scottish accent, and had alert, probing eyes. Alice paused, as though considering. In her mother's absence, she had come down to reception and taken charge, explaining to the raiding party that her mother wouldn't be back until the afternoon.

'I saw him about four weeks ago,' she answered. 'He came back for a mass for my friend's granddad.'

'And you haven't seen him since?' asked the Tan, his eyes boring into Alice.

The man was intimidating, but she forced herself to hold his gaze and speak calmly. 'That's the only time I saw him since he left at the end of September.'

'When he worked here, where did he live?'

'In the staff quarters on the top floor.'

'Right, we need to search there.'

Alice feared that if they went there and found nothing they might want to search other rooms. She tried to make her objection sound reasonable. 'Is there any point searching?' she said. 'He hasn't lived here for months. Why would he come back to a place where he doesn't work any more?'

'Because he's fled and he needs to hide somewhere. And he probably has friends here.' The Tan pointed his finger at Alice. 'Like you, maybe.'

Alice shook her head. 'He was just an employee. He wasn't my friend.' Even though she was lying to protect Johnny, she still felt bad about disowning him.

'Either way, we're searching the place,' said the Scot.

'Can we keep it to the staff quarters? I don't want to upset the guests.'

'I don't give a Highlanders about the guests! Now get the keys.'

'All right,' said Alice, raising her hands to appease the Tan, before turning to the reception desk. 'Could I have the master key, please,

Miss Hopkins?'

The receptionist held out the key, and Alice took it. *She had to try to warn Johnny before the Tans finished on the top floor.*

'OK, here's the master key,' she said, handing it over, 'I'll leave you to it.' Alice turned to walk away but had barely moved when she felt a firm grip on her arm.

'Where do you think you're going?' demanded the Tan.

'I've other work to do.'

'Not now, you haven't. You come with us.'

Alice was about to protest, but she stopped herself, fearing it might sound suspicious to argue too much. 'Fine,' she said. 'If you want to waste everyone's time, let's search the staff quarters.'

Johnny looked in the bathroom mirror, taken aback by his own reflection.

'What do you think?' asked his mother.

'It feels really weird. I…I don't look like myself.'

'That's the general idea.'

His mother had dyed his mop of brown hair black, and plastered it down with oil. Before leaving the chemists shop in Athlone she had acquired the dye, the oil and a pair of glasses with plain lenses, which Johnny now wore.

'Let's see what the others think of you,' suggested his mother.

'OK,' agreed Johnny. He opened the bathroom door and steeped back into the hotel bedroom. He realised that Alice was missing, then his attention was taken by the look of shock on Stella's face.

'Oh my goodness!' she cried, putting her hands to her mouth.

'You like my new look?'

'It's amazing. Great work, Miss Dunne.'

'No point working in a chemist's if you can't get your hands on some bits and bobs,' she said with a smile.

'It's really good,' said Stella, 'but I've some bad news. The Tans arrived while you were doing the dying. Alice is downstairs dealing with them.'

Johnny felt a sinking feeling in his stomach. 'God,' he said. 'What will we do now?'

'We could brazen it out,' said his mother. 'They're looking for a brown-haired boy on his own. They won't be looking for a black-haired boy with glasses who's travelling with his mother.'

'I'd only try that if you have to,' cautioned Stella. 'Alice will do everything she can to misdirect them.'

Johnny could see that his mother wasn't fully convinced.

'Supposing she can't misdirect them?' she said.

'Alice is pretty smart,' answered Stella. 'I think the best thing is to sit tight and trust her.'

'Johnny?' asked his mother.

Johnny bit his lip, thinking hard. His instinct was to make a break, but he knew the Tans would have the hotel surrounded. Following his mother's suggestion would be risky, but could pay off. The authorities didn't have a picture of him, just a description, and with his changed appearance, and travelling as part of a mother and son pairing, they might get away. Then again if they could avoid running the gauntlet that would be better. And Alice *was* smart, maybe she could put the Tans off the scent. He hesitated another moment, trying to think straight, then made up his mind.

'OK,' he said. 'let's stay put, and trust in Alice.'

'I told you he wouldn't be in the hotel,' said Alice.

The Tans had searched all of the staff quarters on the top floor of the Mill, and the Scottish sergeant leading the raid had kept his men in check, with no damage done to the room.

'He could still be in the hotel; we've just ruled out the staff quarters,' answered the Tan.

'Look, Sergeant, I know you've a job to do. But we've a job too, and it's to keep guests happy. Can you search the kitchen and the outhouses and wherever else you want, but not disturb our guests? Please?'

The Tan's expression hardened. 'Do you know why we're looking for this fella?'

'No.'

'He was living in a house full of rebels.'

'But wasn't he just a boarder?'

'Just a boarder? In a place that's a hotbed of Shinners? And when we show up and make arrests, he's vanished. That's not suspicious?'

'There might be a perfectly good explanation.'

'There is. He's *involved*. And twelve of our men were murdered yesterday morning. Anyone involved is going to pay for that.'

Alice felt like saying that fourteen innocent civilians in Croke Park had already paid, but she restrained herself and tried to keep her tone reasonable. 'I understand why you're angry, Sergeant, but let's be realistic. Johnny Dunne is hardly being hidden by hotel guests in a place he worked in months ago.'

The Tan appeared to think about this, then he looked Alice in the eye. 'You could be right. Then again, you could be wrong. But we'll soon find out, won't we?'

'I'm getting worried,' said Johnny. 'If everything was OK, Alice would have come back and told us.'

Stella could understand his nervousness, and she forced herself to sound calm. 'It's only been a few minutes, Johnny. She's probably still talking to the Tans.'

'Or unlocking doors for them, if they're searching room-to-room,' suggested Miss Dunne.

'If she is, it's only because they made her,' insisted Stella.

'I know,' said Johnny. 'But if they *do* make her, we're trapped here like fish in a barrel.'

'Maybe we should just brazen it out,' said Miss Dunne. 'I know it's risky, but so is being found here with our bags packed.'

Stella thought for a moment, then reached a decision. 'I've a better idea.'

Johnny looked at her hopefully. 'What?'

'Move to my room,' suggested Stella. 'The Tans won't know we're friends. If they're told my room is the permanent quarters of a British officer's daughter, there'd be no reason to search it.'

'That's not guaranteed, Stella,' said Miss Dunne.

'Nothing's guaranteed. But I reckon your chances are better in my room.' Stella hoped that her argument had swayed Miss Dunne, who now turned to her son.

'What do you say, Johnny?'

'There's a risk either way. But I think…I think Stella's right. Being in a room hired by Commander Radcliffe might be our best bet.'

'Can we get there without going through the lobby?' asked Miss Dunne.

Stella nodded. 'Yes, we can go by the back stairs.'

'All right,' said Johnny, reaching for his suitcase. 'Let's do it.'

'I'll just check there's no one in the corridor,' said Stella. She opened the bedroom door and stepped out. To her relief there was nobody about, and she stepped back into room nine. 'The coast's clear. Let's go!'

Alice was trying hard to appear pleasant and helpful. The Tans had searched all the outhouses and storerooms and were now going through the kitchen. She had told the hotel staff to be co-operative and had even offered the Tans refreshments, which the Scottish sergeant had politely refused. Alice felt that she had won him over a little, but the real test would come if he still insisted on searching all the hotel bedrooms.

Alice's fall-back position would be the suggestion that they check every room that had been vacated, but respect the privacy of guests in rooms that were occupied.

'All clear in the kitchen, Sarge,' reported one of the Tans, returning to the lobby.

'Right, the rooms are next.'

'Can I talk to you about that, Sergeant, please?' said Alice.

'We've already talked about it.'

Alice was about to make her case when her eye was caught by movement at the entrance door. To her surprise she saw Commander Radcliffe and Mrs Radcliffe approaching. They were back ahead of schedule, which could spell disaster. Presumably they would look for Stella. And if they found her with Johnny and his mother the game would be up. Before Alice could think it through any further they approached. Stella's father was in his RAF uniform and the Scottish sergeant saluted him respectfully.

'Wing Commander.'

'Sergeant. What's going on here?'

'Premises search, sir.'

'They're looking for Johnny Dunne, Commander,' said Alice. 'They have this notion that he's involved with the rebels. I told them that none of us have seen him in a month, and we know nothing about him ever being involved with the rebels.' Alice looked at Stella's father meaningfully. They both knew that Johnny had probably saved his life yesterday morning. Now Alice held her breath, praying that Commander Radcliffe would return the favour and sing dumb.

'Can you do a Yankee accent, Mam?' asked Johnny.

They were seated in Stella's room, which they had reached without incident, although everyone was still on edge.

His mother looked at him bemusedly. 'An American accent? Well, yes, I did one in a sketch once, in the Town Hall in Athlone. Why do you ask?'

'If the Tans come in here we could pretend we're Canadian friends of Stella's.'

Johnny was rewarded with an approving nod from his mother. 'That's a really good idea.'

Stella looked slightly concerned. 'The accent isn't exactly the same.'

'It's close enough,' said Johnny. 'The Tans hardly know the difference between an American and a Canadian accent.'

'No, I suppose not,' Stella admitted.

'We could claim to be friends from Ontario, getting the train to Dublin this afternoon,' continued Johnny. He remembered the approach adopted by Mr O'Shea and by Michael Collins, and decided that he and his mother should have a back story. 'How do we know you, Stella? And where would be a good place to come from, just in case it comes up?'

Stella thought a moment. 'Why don't we stay with the chess club? Say that's where we met when we both lived in Toronto?'

'Where in Toronto?' asked Johnny.

'Yorkville,' answered Stella. 'We were neighbours. We lived on Admiral Road and you lived on...let's say Lowther Avenue. All right?'

'OK.' Johnny looked enquiringly at his mother, who nodded.

'Fine' she said, 'Yorkville, Admiral Road, Lowther Avenue.'

Johnny thought of the other things that had impressed him the night he had been questioned with Michael Collins, and he turned to his mother. 'If it comes to bluffing our way as Canadians, the trick is to act as though we're completely at ease.'

'You've done stuff like this before?' she asked.

'A bit, yes. So if we're questioned, we haven't a worry in the world. We're for the authorities, we know they're doing what they have to, and we're confident that soon we'll be on our way.'

'You make it sound easy, Johnny,' said Stella.

'My heart is beating like a drum, but they don't know that. Mr O'Shea always says that people take you at your own valuation. Act innocent and you seem innocent.'

'Fair enough,' said Johnny's mother, 'though I'm praying it won't arise.'

'Absolutely,' said Stella. 'Let's just hope...'

But what she hoped for never got said, as all three of them started, on hearing a knock on the bedroom door.

Johnny swallowed hard. He prayed that his disguise and their concocted story would be enough, and he watched anxiously as Stella rose and opened the door.

'Mom! Dad!' she cried in surprise as Commander and Mrs Radcliffe stepped into the room.

Alice accompanied the Tans, a master key in her hand as they arrived at the first bedroom on the ground floor. Perspiration had formed on her brow, and she wiped it away surreptitiously, as she prepared to make a final argument to prevent Johnny being found.

'I really, think, Sergeant—'

'Shut it!' snapped the Tan. 'We won't disturb your precious guests more than we have to, but we're searching each room. Now look lively and start opening up.'

Alice felt her heart sink, but she couldn't think of any response.

'Come on! The sooner we do this, the sooner it ends.'

Alice was afraid to delay any further. Instead she breathed out wearily and inserted the key in the lock of room one.

'I can explain everything,' said Stella.

'You'd better!' said her father.

'Mom, Dad, this is Miss Dunne. Miss Dunne, my mother, Mrs Louise Radcliffe, and my father, Wing Commander Bernard Radcliffe.'

Despite the bizarre circumstances, the adults exchanged brief how-do-you-dos.

'And of course you know Johnny,' said Stella, 'despite the dyed hair and the glasses.'

'Yes, we know Johnny,' replied her mother. 'What's he doing in your bedroom?'

'He's avoiding the Tans,' answered Stella.

'God above, Stella!' said her father. 'Have you any idea what you're playing at?!'

'Yes, Dad,' she answered, trying to keep her voice calm. 'I'm helping the best friend I ever had. He's finally found his mother,' she said, pointing at Miss Dunne, 'and they want to start a new life in Scotland.'

'His mother?' Stella could tell from her tone that Mom was confused. '*Miss Dunne*?'

'Yes,' answered Johnny's mother. 'It's a long, complicated story, but Johnny is my son, and now we want to make a fresh start. I'm sorry that you and your family should be embroiled in it all.'

'So well you might be,' said Commander Radcliffe.

'Dad, please,' said Stella.

'Do you realise there's a truckload of Tans searching the hotel for Johnny right now?' he said. 'They could arrive here any minute, Stella. Have you any idea of the danger that puts us all in?'

'Yes, Dad, I have. And I'm really scared. But it's still less than the danger that Johnny put himself into yesterday morning. You might be dead now if it wasn't for what he did.'

To his credit, she saw that her father looked abashed.

'I am, of course, hugely grateful to you, Johnny,' he said.

'That's OK, Commander.'

'No it's not OK. You took an enormous risk, and I'll be forever thankful. But you were also involved in an operation that ended up with twelve of my colleagues dead. I can't just write that off.'

'Fourteen civilians were dead after Croke Park,' said Stella.

'I know that, love, and it's appalling. But I still have a duty. I took an oath of allegiance to the King.'

'May I say something?' said Miss Dunne, and Stella looked at her, curious to hear her view.

'You mightn't like his cause, Commander, but Johnny had a duty, as he saw it. And he had an allegiance too. But for your sake he put it on hold. Can you not do the same? The fight is over for Johnny. Couldn't you let a fourteen-year-old boy leave the country, to make a new start?'

Stella could see that her father was conflicted. Johnny and Miss Dunne looked anxious, but said nothing further, and Stella's mother, who had been listening carefully, opened her mouth to speak. Before she got a word out, however, there was a sharp knock on the door. Stella felt her stomach constricting in fear. Then she rose at once as she heard the heard a key being inserted into the lock.

Alice opened the door to Stella's room and started in shock. 'Stella!' she said. She had expected her friend to be upstairs in room nine. Instead she got a glimpse into the room and saw Johnny and Miss Dunne, as well as Commander and Mrs Radcliffe. Johnny looked different with black hair and glasses, but it was the presence of Commander Radcliffe that gave Alice a ray of hope.

Acting on instinct, she blocked the door with her body and turned to the Scottish sergeant. 'Wing Commander Radcliffe is in the room with his daughter. Clearly you won't need to search it now.'

The Tan seemed to consider this, then he spoke firmly. 'Stand aside.'

'Really, Sergeant, he's a British officer, so surely...'

'Surely nothing! I say where we search. Now stand aside.'

The sergeant was carrying a Webley revolver and was backed up by heavily-armed Tans, and Alice knew that defying him was pointless. Sickened to think of what lay ahead, she slowly stepped aside.

Johnny felt his pulses throbbing as the leader of the Tans, a sergeant, stepped into the room. He was followed by Alice and two of the other Tans, and although Stella's bedroom was spacious, it was beginning to feel crowded.

'We meet again, sir,' said the sergeant. 'I'm sorry to disturb you, but you'll understand that every room must be checked.'

'Quite,' answered Commander Radcliffe.

Johnny watched the RAF officer anxiously, trying to get a clue from his expression as to whether or not he would turn them in. Before Commander Radcliffe could say anything further, Johnny's mother stepped forward, smilingly offering her hand for the Tan to shake.

'Felicity Mackenzie,' she said in a convincing North American accent.

The Tan looked slightly taken aback, but instinctively shook the proferred hand.

'Sergeant Morris,' he replied.

'And this is my son, Wilfred,' said Johnny's mother.

Johnny gathered himself, then spoke up in the most convincing American accent he could produce. 'How do you do, sir.'

Johnny sensed that the Tan wasn't used to such courtesy during raids, and the man seemed a little surprised, but nodded back in greeting. Johnny was impressed by his mother's initiative and grateful now for the hair dye and the glasses.

'Can I ask what you're doing here, Ma'am?' said the Tan.

Johnny's mother indicated the Radcliffes. 'Saying goodbye to our old Yorkville neighbours, before travelling back to Canada. We were just about to say our farewells and head for the Dublin train, right, Wilf?'

'Sure thing, Mom,' answered Johnny in his American accent, using an expression he had heard from Stella.

'Right,' said the Tan. 'Although…you don't sound Canadian, sir,' he said, turning to Commander Radcliffe.

Johnny swallowed hard. If Stella's father was going to give them up, now was the moment. He could see Stella looking appealingly at him, but Johnny sensed from Commander Radcliffe's demeanour that he was unsure about what to do.

For a second nobody spoke, and the agony of indecision seemed like an eternity to Johnny. Then, to his surprise, Stella's mother intervened.

'My husband is English, Sergeant, I'm the Canadian one,' she said with a pleasant smile.

'I see.'

'Mrs Mackenzie and Wilfred were on holidays in Ireland, so we've been catching up on old times.'

Johnny felt hugely relieved and wanted to hug Mrs Radcliffe in gratitude. Then he looked back at Stella's father. The tight expression on his face told Johnny that as a British officer he struggled with the thought of helping an enemy of the Crown to escape.

'Wilfred was a great friend to Stella,' continued Mrs Radcliffe, 'and indeed to the family. Wasn't he, Bernard?' she said looking her husband in the eye.

Johnny knew that she was reminding him of what had happened at The Eastwood Hotel and he held his breath, unsure how Stella's father would respond. There was a short pause, although again it seemed to Johnny to stretch interminably. Then Commander Radcliffe nodded curtly.

'Yes, Wilfred was a true blue,' he said.

Johnny felt like pumping his fist in victory, but settled for a modest smile of acknowledgement. 'Thank you, Commander,' he answered. He felt a flood of relief coursing through his system and had to tell himself not to relax – that they still had to talk their way out of the room.

'So, you're Stella?' said the Tan, turning to face her.

'Yes.'

'And you would have known Johnny Dunne?'

'Yes, we were friends.'

'Friends?'

'Well, we were in the same band, and we lived under the same roof, so we became pals.'

Johnny was surprised that Stella wasn't playing down her association with him, and he wondered what her game was.

'When was the last time you saw him?' asked the Tan.

'About a month ago.'

The Tan looked at her directly. 'You're sure you haven't spoken to him since then?'

'That was the last time I saw him, but I spoke to him today,' said Stella.'

'What?'

'He rang me from Dublin to say a final goodbye. He was getting the train to Queenstown and then the boat to America.'

Johnny realised that Stella was deliberately laying a false trail, and he felt a surge of affection for her.

'When was this telephone call?' asked the Tan excitedly.

'Earlier this morning.'

He turned to his men. 'Private Barrett!'

'Sarge?'

'Go to reception and get on the phone. Put out an alert for Johnny Dunne at Queenstown. Both the train station and the harbour.'

'Yes, sarge,' said the man, hurrying from the room.

'Why are you looking for Johnny?' asked Stella innocently.

'You didn't know he was involved with the rebels?' said the Tan.

'No! Gosh. That's…that's terrible.'

Stella looked genuinely shocked, and Johnny was impressed both by her coolness and her acting skills.

'We're eager to talk to him,' said the Tan, then he turned from Stella and addressed her father. 'Forgive me, sir, but for form's sake you'll understand that we complete our search of the hotel. Including a quick search of these quarters.'

'If you must,' said Commander Radcliffe.

At a nod from the sergeant the other Tans moved to begin checking the bathroom and the wardrobes.

'Well, we'll say our farewells,' said Johnny's mother, and she kissed Mrs Radcliffe on the cheek, then shook hands with her husband.

Johnny followed suit, and Commander Radcliff locked eyes with him as they shook hands. There was a charged moment, with each of them aware of the risks that they had taken on each other's behalf. Then Commander Radcliffe gave a quick nod, which Johnny returned.

'Goodbye, Wilfred,' said Alice. 'And the very best of luck back in Canada. It's been great meeting you.'

Even though she was trying to keep her tone light, as befitting a goodbye to a boy she didn't know well, Johnny could hear the emotion in her voice. He wished that they could have a proper farewell, but he had to settle for squeezing her hand as he shook it.

'Thanks, Alice,' he said warmly. 'You've…you've helped make my stay really special.'

'Safe trip, Wilf,' said Stella, approaching.

'Thanks for everything, Stella,' answered Johnny, looking at her meaningfully and trying to convey just how much he meant it. He could see a hint of tears welling up in her eyes and he felt a lump in his own throat. He squeezed hard as they shook hands, then Stella quickly reached out and hugged him. 'Safe journey, Johnny,' she whispered. 'You're a great friend.'

'You too, Stella,' he answered, then they separated, and Johnny turned away, afraid that his eyes too might well up.

His mother said goodbye to the girls, then lifted her suitcase and turned back to him.

'OK, Wilf, time to go.'

Johnny lifted his suitcase also, but saw the sergeant looking at him quizzically.

'Are you making for the train station?' asked the Tan.

Johnny felt his throat going dry. *For things to go wrong now would be unbearable.* 'Yes,' he said trying to sound unworried. 'Catching the Dublin train'.

'You're walking to the station? Carrying all that luggage?'

Johnny hesitated, unsure how to respond.

'Gosh no!' said his mother with a light laugh. 'I'm not a pack horse, sergeant! The hotel porter will take it from reception.'

Johnny prayed that this would satisfy the Tan, though it was hard to tell from his face what he was thinking.

'Right,' said the Tan. 'Well in that case, I'll wish you a safe journey.'

'Thank you, sergeant.'

Johnny breathed out in silent relief, then there was a flurry of final farewells and he followed his mother out the door. He felt sad to leave his friends, but thrilled to have fooled the Tans, and he walked briskly along the corridor, eager to make his getaway.

CHAPTER TWENTY-FOUR

'It'll never be the same again, Alice,' said Stella.

They were in their pyjamas and seated before a glowing coal fire in Stella's bedroom.

'Without Johnny?'

'Yes. I know he's been living in Dublin. But going to Glasgow – it feels more permanent.'

'If he gets to Glasgow.'

'I think he will. The Tans are looking for him down in Queenstown. A Canadian mother and son crossing from Belfast to Stranraer shouldn't draw attention.'

'You're right, we should be positive,' said Alice firmly, then she sipped her mug of cocoa. 'It's been a crazy few days, hasn't it?'

'Terrifying,' answered Stella, thinking back to her father's near miss in The Eastwood Hotel, and the subsequent slaughter that they were calling Bloody Sunday. The fallout was still going on, and after the Tans had finished their search of the hotel, Dad had agreed that Mom would stay overnight in an adjacent room in the Mill, to be with Stella until things settled down. He had had to return to Baldonnel, and so there had been no time to discuss the compromises with their beliefs that both Dad and Johnny had made.

'I'm really glad Mam was in Rush when the Tans came today,'

said Alice, breaking Stella's reverie.

'What, you think she'd have turned Johnny in?'

Alice grimaced. 'I honestly don't know. She's never been keen on him. And she's furious that he brought the Tans down on us. But I'd still like to think that she wouldn't have sold him out.'

'I don't think she would. But it's best she doesn't know the truth.'

'No, she'd have a fit,' said Alice. 'I don't like keeping secrets, but this time what she doesn't know, won't worry her.'

'I wonder how it will all end,' said Stella.

Alice sipped her mug and shrugged. 'Who knows?'

'Looking back, I can't believe the last two years.'

'Yeah?'

'Meeting you, meeting Johnny, playing in the band, seeing Balbriggan being burnt down. If I live to be ninety I won't forget this time.'

'You say that like it's coming to a close.'

'I don't know what Dad's plans are. But I don't think Mom is eager to stay here after what nearly happened to Dad.'

'So you might be going away too?

'I hope not, Alice, I love it here. But who can say?'

'It's bad enough losing Johnny. If you go as well it'll be awful.'

'Then let's not think about it. We'll cross our bridges if we come to them.'

'OK.'

'And when all this is over maybe Johnny can come back, and

we can all be friends again.'

'I'd love that,' said Alice.

'To you, me and Johnny then,' said Stella, smiling and raising her mug in a toast.

Alice raised her mug and smiled back. 'To you, me and Johnny!'

The ship came gradually to a halt, and within minutes thick ropes were cast ashore and tied, and a gangplank lowered. The sea air had a sting to it, but Johnny had come out on deck earlier, wanting to see the moonlit Scottish coastline as the ship approached the port of Stranraer. Now the brightly lit dockside was alive with activity as the first passengers made their way down the gangplank and onto the quayside.

Johnny watched carefully, on the lookout for police officers – either uniformed or in plain clothes – but none of the foot passengers who streamed off the boat was stopped, and there seemed to be no police presence.

'I think it's going to be OK,' he said to his mother, who stood beside him.

'I think so too,' she answered with a smile.

In fact, everything had gone smoothly once they left behind the Tans in the Mill. With their train tickets already bought, they had boarded the train for Belfast unchallenged. Johnny reckoned that Stella's invented story had focussed attention on the County

Cork port of Cobh, and no one in Belfast had paid them attention, either at the train station or the ferry terminal.

Even so, his mother had suggested that they exit the ship in Stranraer when the quayside was at its busiest. *His mother.* He still loved being able to use the term, and he looked at her now, her profile lit by the dockside illumination. Once again he was struck by how much he looked like her. He thought that it was magical that there was someone else in the world with similar features to his, and that it was a small miracle that they had found each other after all this time.

She turned to him now and caught him staring at her. 'What?' she said with a quizzical smile?

'Nothing,' said Johnny, 'I'm...I'm just glad we're going to be together.'

'Me too, Johnny,' she said simply. 'Me too.'

Johnny was touched by the affection in her tone. 'Thanks, Mam,' he said. 'But, eh…time to go, I think,' he said, indicating the quayside and picking up his suitcase.

'Yes, it looks all clear.'

His mother took up her case also and they made their way to the gang plank. Now that they were almost on Scottish soil he found himself thinking of those he had left behind in Ireland. He hoped that Mrs Hanlon wouldn't be mistreated in custody, and that Mr O'Shea would evade the Tans. He hoped too that Alice and Stella wouldn't get in trouble with their parents or be linked to his rebel activities. But he had been really careful all along not to leave any evidence that would implicate his friends, and he told himself that they would be safe. And finally he hoped that they could all be together again as soon as possible. Alice and Stella had been the best finds he had ever had, and he would miss them.

But now he was about to begin a fresh chapter in his life. He would be part of a family and he would get to know better his mother, and his uncle and aunt, and his cousins. He had been given an opportunity that he had never expected, and he was determined to make the most of it.

He reached the end of the gangplank and stepped down onto the quayside. His mother looked at him and smiled, then held out her free hand. Johnny smiled back and took her hand, then he walked off into the night, and the start of his new life.